"Is someth

"Everything's fine. That'll be fun. The birthday, I mean. Um…" Sam had to know. "When is it?"

"December fifteenth."

Sam struggled to stay calm, even though the date knocked the breath out of her. Of all the bizarre coincidences, William and her son—*both* of AJ's sons—were born on the same day. There was no longer any doubt that he'd been sleeping with her and William's mother at the same time. Still, for his wife to have a baby on the same day she did… it was crazy.

What if…?

You're the one who's crazy. There's no way William is your son.

Unless…had AJ found out she was pregnant?

Snippets of recent events flashed through her mind. AJ had been reluctant to take them into the kitchen that first day, when Will was out in the yard. He was awkward and edgy when she and Will were in the same room together. Was it because he felt guilty for cheating on his wife? Or was it something even more underhanded?

Dear Reader,

The Christmas Secret combines all of my favorite things in one story—a woman with an untraditional career, a single dad, a secret baby, a puppy and, of course, Christmas! The real inspiration for this book, though, was my love of home-and-garden shows on television. DIY, home decorating, real estate—I love them all! So I thought, why not combine them into one business? Ready Set Sold is that business and it's owned by three women—a carpenter, an interior decorator and a real-estate agent.

When Andrew "AJ" Harris hires Ready Set Sold to sell the house he inherited from his grandmother, he is unexpectedly reunited with Samantha Elliott, the only woman he's ever loved, the woman he's never been able to forget and the woman whose betrayal he can never forgive.

Sam has been keeping a secret and she's sure that if AJ ever finds out, he'll never forgive her. What she doesn't know is that AJ has a secret, too, and now that Sam is temporarily back in his life, keeping that secret from her becomes all-important, not just for his sake but for their son's.

I hope you enjoy Sam and AJ's journey as they discover that once all the secrets are out in the open, love and forgiveness go hand in hand. I love to hear from readers, so I also hope you'll visit me at my website, www.leemckenzie.com.

Happy holidays!

Lee McKenzie

The Christmas Secret

LEE MCKENZIE

TORONTO NEW YORK LONDON
AMSTERDAM PARIS SYDNEY HAMBURG
STOCKHOLM ATHENS TOKYO MILAN MADRID
PRAGUE WARSAW BUDAPEST AUCKLAND

Recycling programs
for this product may
not exist in your area.

ISBN-13: 978-0-373-75384-0

THE CHRISTMAS SECRET

ABOUT THE AUTHOR

From the time she was ten years old and read *Anne of Green Gables* and *Little Women*, Lee McKenzie knew she wanted to be a writer, just like Anne and Jo. In the intervening years, she has written everything from advertising copy to an honors thesis in paleontology, but becoming a four-time Golden Heart finalist and a Harlequin author are among her proudest accomplishments. Lee and her artist/teacher husband live on an island along Canada's west coast, and she loves to spend time with two of her best friends—her grown-up children.

Books by Lee McKenzie

HARLEQUIN AMERICAN ROMANCE
1167—THE MAN FOR MAGGIE
1192—WITH THIS RING
1316—FIREFIGHTER DADDY
1340—THE WEDDING BARGAIN

For Joe

Chapter One

Grandmother Harris's backyard was a perfect place for a little boy and his dog to play. AJ Harris walked out onto the deck, coffee in hand, in time to see his son romp across the lawn with their chocolate-colored Labradoodle puppy in hot pursuit, both under the watchful eye of his nanny, Annie Dobson. He left the door ajar so he could hear the doorbell when it rang and went down the steps to join them.

"Taking a break, Mr. Harris?" Annie asked. She was sitting in one of the old Adirondacks that had been in this yard for as long as he could remember, steam rising from her teacup into the cool morning air.

"That's one of the best things about working at home. I can take a break whenever I want." The best part, though, was being his own boss instead of one of his father's employees.

"Daddy! I playing with Hawshey!"

"I *am* playing with Hershey," he said.

"Sam-I-*am!*" His son shouted the name from his favorite book, then stopped running and flung himself on the grass, laughing and shrieking when the puppy pounced on him.

"William! Don't let that creature lick your face."

Annie's reprimand was firm but gentle. "You've seen what else he licks. For goodness' sake, think of the germs!"

AJ sat in the chair next to hers and set his cup on the arm. The boy and his dog were up and running again and the sound of Will's laughter lightened AJ's mood in a way nothing else could.

"I appreciate you bringing them out here to play," he said. "I would have taken them to the park like I usually do, but the real estate people will be here any minute."

"A little fresh air never hurt an old lady like me, either, and it's a nice day for late November." Annie sipped her tea. "I'll miss this old place."

So would he. His earliest and certainly happiest memories were of times spent here. He hated having to sell the house, but it was the best option. Hell, it was his only option. Grandmother Harris was gone, his only other family ties in Seattle were his parents, and they hadn't spoken to him since the day he'd brought his son home from the hospital. And for the past three years he'd felt as though he was holding his breath and hoping his past didn't catch up to him.

He was looking forward to a fresh start, and for that he needed the money from this inheritance. He and his son would build a new life in Idaho, in a community where being "a Harris" meant nothing. Where there was no possibility of running into his family, and no possibility of a chance encounter with the woman who had selfishly abandoned their son.

His main reason for leaving the city, though, was William. The little boy had recently taken an interest in mothers from a story they'd read. In a few years he would start asking about *his* mother, maybe even wanting to see her. Best to leave now, before Will was old enough to wonder about the woman who had brought him into the world, before his early childhood in Seattle became fixed in his memory. When he finally did ask, AJ had no idea what he would tell him, but that day was a long way off. At least he hoped it was. He swore it would be the only time he would ever lie to his son, but he would have to. No child needed to know that his own mother hadn't wanted him.

He and Will would miss Annie Dobson, too, but she had no desire to move to a cabin on the outskirts of a small town in Idaho, and who could blame her? Besides, it was probably time she thought about retirement.

The doorbell's four chimes, one slightly off-key, pulled his attention back to the present.

"I'll keep young William and the puppy out here so they're not underfoot," Annie said.

"Thanks. I appreciate that. When this meeting is over, I'll take them off your hands for a while."

This real estate company had been referred to him by a magazine editor who'd bought a couple of free-lance articles from him last month. He'd met with a Ms. DeAngelo earlier in the week, had been impressed with her businesslike efficiency and had signed the contract and hired her on the spot. This morning she was bringing her "team of professionals" from Ready Set Sold to inspect the house. His grandmother's century-old craftsman home was situated in Seattle's fashionable Queen Anne neighborhood overlooking Lake Union, but after years of neglect that's all it had going for it. Ms. DeAngelo—he couldn't remember her first name—had assured him her company would make the necessary upgrades and repairs, and "stage the house for today's market." They would even help him figure out what to do with his grandmother's personal belongings.

Inside the kitchen, he closed the creaky French doors and walked through the dining room and living room, past many decades' worth of furniture and bric-a-brac—some antique and some not so antique—and into the foyer. He opened the door and slammed headlong into his past.

Samantha Elliott, Will's mother, the one woman whose betrayal he would never forget, or forgive, stood on the veranda. A multitude of emotions tore through him. Resentment, distrust, disgust, but in the end fear won out. The deadweight of it actually squeezed the air out of his lungs. For the past three years he'd lived under a dark cloud, determined to keep his secret. Why, when he was so close to escaping Seattle and his past, did some Machiavellian twist of fate have to deliver up the one person who had the power to take it all away?

"AJ?" The surprise in her voice matched his. She stepped back, checked the numbers above the door and consulted the clipboard she was carrying.

Was it possible she was at the wrong house? That perhaps the Fates were merely playing a devious practical joke?

"Sam." He immediately regretted saying her name out loud. It made her being there a reality when he desperately wanted it to be a trick of his imagination. "What do you want?" He hated to ask but had to know.

She handed him a business card.

Selling your home?
Looking to get top dollar in today's competitive
real estate market?
Call Samantha Elliott at READY SET SOLD
1-800-555-SOLD
www.Ready-Set-Sold.net

The card was identical to the one Ms. DeAngelo had given him, except for where it said *Call Samantha Elliott.*

"I'm one of the owners of Ready Set Sold. We've been hired to get this house ready to sell. Is this…?" Her voice trailed off the way it often had, leaving her thoughts unspoken.

His fear downgraded to anxiety. She didn't know his secret. That's not why she was here. "It's my grand-mother's house. It *was*. She left it to me."

"Oh. I'm sorry. About your grandmother, I mean. Not the house." She glanced back at the street, then at her watch. "Um…I'm meeting my business partners here. I guess I'm early. I can wait…" A car door slammed and Sam looked relieved. "Oh, good. Here's Claire."

Right. Claire. The woman he'd met earlier in the week walked briskly up the front sidewalk and climbed the stairs, confident in spite of her high heels. Sam, he noticed, was wearing work boots. Toes reinforced with steel, no doubt. Just like her heart.

Claire extended her hand. "Mr. Harris. Hello. Nice to see you again. I see you've already met our carpenter, Samantha Elliott. Kristi Callahan, our interior decora-tor, should be here any minute."

He accepted her handshake. "Please, call me AJ. Mr. Harris is my father."

Sam's blue eyes went icy at the mention of the old man. He couldn't fault her for that.

An old white minivan in desperate need of a muffler pulled up and sputtered to a stop behind the dark blue truck and the silver-gray sedan already parked in front of the house. All three vehicles had the Ready Set Sold logo on their doors.

The third woman joined them, and Claire introduced

her. "AJ Harris, this is Kristi Callahan, decorator extraordinaire."

AJ was suddenly overwhelmed with a feeling of being…overwhelmed. This was a bad idea. A very bad one. Not in a million years would he have hired this company if he'd known Sam was one of the owners. He should have done his homework, checked out their website, something. Instead he had been swayed by Claire DeAngelo's no-nonsense approach and businesslike demeanor. Her company would take care of everything and he would walk away with enough cash for him and his son to start a new life, well away from the woman who had just barged into his old one.

"We'll do a walk-through this morning," Claire said. "After we've done the inspection, we'll prepare a list of the repairs and upgrades needed and come up with a design plan for staging the house."

It all sounded so easy, except he knew now those repairs would be done by Sam.

"Should we get started?" Claire asked.

He looked at Sam again and felt himself drawn into her soft, doe-eyed gaze. She was beautiful and he hated her for it. He wanted to say no, he'd changed his mind and would come up with another plan for selling the house, yet his latent curiosity wanted to keep her here. Find out if maybe she had changed. It was foolhardy and dangerous, but he hadn't felt this alive since the last time he'd been with her.

He stepped aside, allowing the three women into his home and Samantha Elliott back into his life.

SAMANTHA RELUCTANTLY followed her two business partners inside. She really needed to pay more attention to the business end of the company. If she had, she would have known they'd been hired by Andrew James Harris of *the* Seattle Harris family, and she could have put a stop to it *before* he signed the contract. The last time she'd worked for him had not ended well, and this new undertaking had disaster written all over it.

Still, she assured herself, the past was the past and there was no way AJ could discover the secret she'd buried with it. The only other person who knew the truth was her mother, and anyone acquainted with Tildy Elliott would never believe the story. They would assume it was simply one of the many delusions that governed Tildy's life.

You'll be okay, Sam told herself. Besides, Claire and Kristi always had her back. If the situation got out of hand, she'd convince them to hire another carpenter for this job. That meant she'd have to tell them about her ill-fated affair with AJ Harris, but she wouldn't have to tell them everything.

Now, with AJ within arm's reach and as unattainable as ever, she was still struggling to overcome the shock of having him open the door. Three years ago she had been desperately in love with him, thought they were perfect together. Her sorry excuse for a life had made it easy to relate to his tall, dark and tortured disposition. What little they had shared about their pasts had forged a deep, emotional connection between them... or so she'd thought at the time. But he was AJ Harris of *the* Seattle Harrises and she was Samantha Nobody. A reality his father had zeroed in on in the cruelest way possible and one that AJ had agreed with, leaving her to cope with the aftermath of their affair...alone.

"Let's start right here in the foyer," Claire said. "The millwork is in unbelievably good condition and it's never been painted. The whole house is like this, right?"

AJ nodded.

"What do you think, Kristi? I know the current trend is to paint the trim, but the natural wood suits this old craftsman architecture."

Kristi, camera in hand, was already taking photographs. "I agree. Once the wallpaper's been stripped and we give the walls a fresh coat of paint—I'm seeing ivory or off-white—this room will feel brighter and more spacious. I love this old oak hall tree, too. It should stay but we'll get rid of a lot of the clutter and replace all these scatter mats with a runner." She lowered her camera for a moment. "I love this banister. With the holidays coming, I'll stage the house for Christmas." She looped the camera strap around her neck and made a wide, sweeping gesture at the staircase. "Faux greenery, big red velvet bows—it'll be stunning."

"Great idea. What are your thoughts, Sam?"

Sam thought she should make a run for it. Clearly not what Claire had in mind. And as for Christmas… bah humbug. "Taking down the wallpaper will be easy, and I can install a new light fixture, too. This one isn't original and really doesn't suit the house."

AJ, who stood with both hands shoved in the pockets of his black jeans, looked up at the ceiling and studied the out-of-place pendant as though seeing it for the first time. Then he looked at Sam. Their gazes locked and held, and a rush of long-dormant lust uncoiled in her belly.

This was not good.

AJ looked away, but she knew he'd felt it, too. Judging by the way Claire was eyeing them, even she'd picked up on it. Great. Now this would be a hot topic at their weekly business meeting tomorrow morning. Sam wouldn't have to tell them everything. Only that she and their new client had once had a brief affair followed by a messy breakup.

Kristi, focused on the monitor of her camera and the offending light fixture, was oblivious to everything else. "Got it," she said. "Okay, that's it for this room."

With shaky hands Sam scrawled a reminder on her clipboard to check the storage facility for old light fixtures. She'd picked up several at a demolition sale last winter and one of them might work here.

"We can discuss the living and dining rooms later," Claire said. "Let's move on to the kitchen. From what I remember when I was here the other day, that room and the main bath upstairs need the most work."

Just her lousy luck, Sam thought. Those were the rooms that took the longest to renovate, which meant this job could take a while. She shot another hasty glance at AJ, in time to catch a flash of panic. Hmm. There was something in the kitchen he didn't want them to see, and Sam knew with absolute certainty it was more than a sink full of dirty dishes. Claire was already on her way, though, so they trooped through the house behind her.

Sam hung back and tried to ignore AJ's presence while she took in the room. The kitchen wasn't great, but it wasn't bad, either. The cabinets were dated, but fresh paint and new hardware would fix that. The appliances were relatively new, but the gold-flecked countertop and starburst-patterned linoleum screamed seventies. They definitely had to be replaced.

Kristi was already taking photographs. "There's way too much clutter," she said, then she lowered her camera and smiled at AJ. "Sorry, but having all these canisters and gadgets on display makes the room feel much smaller than it is. We want potential buyers to walk in and immediately see a place for their espresso machine instead of thinking their things will never work in here."

AJ shrugged. "All these things belonged to my grandmother. I would have cleared everything out, but I wasn't sure what to do with them."

Kristi flashed a reassuring smile. "That's what we're here for," she said. "By the time we're finished, it'll be a brand-new kitchen." She fingered the floral curtains on the kitchen window. "Vintage. Good shape, too." Then something outside seemed to catch her attention. "Oh, what an adorable little boy. Is that your son?"

Sam's heart thundered in her chest. AJ had a child?

Chapter Two

Brimming with anger and overcome with grief, Sam steadied herself by leaning against the door frame.

Breathe, she told herself. *Just breathe. You can get through this.*

AJ's nod in response to Kristi's question was almost imperceptible. He didn't look at Sam, but she still detected the same raw emotion that had greeted her at the door, along with the panic she'd seen when Claire suggested they come in here.

"How old is he?" Kristi asked. "Three? Four?"

AJ still wouldn't look at Sam, and she couldn't have torn her gaze away from him if she tried. "No," he said. "He's…ah…just two."

Two. AJ had a two-year-old son. Which meant he must have a wife. A wife who was probably already married to him when he'd been sleeping with Sam. Which meant he'd been busy getting his wife pregnant while Sam had grappled with the decision to give her son a better life than she ever could.

Oh, God. She couldn't breathe. Her heart raced as scenes from the past flashed through her mind at a dizzying pace, ending with AJ's father. James Harris had said his son had a history of getting involved with

women like her and then dumping them. She hadn't
believed him, even told him as much, but that hadn't
ended the conversation. He'd said that if she kept seeing
AJ, he would put her out of business. Then he'd followed
up that threat by saying her mother needed to be insti-
tutionalized and asking if she was prepared to do that.
Blindsided—how in hell had he found out about her
mother?—Sam knew then he wasn't just a dangerous
man, he was evil. Her life was already hard enough,
and she thought being in love was supposed to make it
easier.

Ending things with AJ had been the easy part. He
had accepted it with a dismissive shrug, exactly like the
one his father had given her when she said putting her
mother in an institution wasn't an option. Like father,
like son? She hadn't completely believed it then, but she
did now.

A month later she suspected she might be pregnant,
and by the time she'd moved past the denial and finally
saw a doctor, she was further along than she'd realized.
She couldn't abandon her mother, but neither could she
raise a child in the unstable environment she'd grown
up in. The rest was inevitable.

"He's adorable. Cute dog, too." As usual, Kristi was
oblivious to the elephant in the room. "He looks tall for
his age. Must get that from his dad."

AJ looked as though he wished she would stop talking. Sam sure as hell did.

"What about your wife?" Kristi asked, still not picking up on the tension. "Will she mind having us in the
way?"

AJ's eyes darted in Sam's direction, but he looked
away before his gaze met hers.

Coward, she thought. Two-timing bastard.

"My…ah…she doesn't live here. I have a nanny who takes care of…us. And the house. She's outside right now with…ah…you'll meet her later."

Claire, who never missed a trick, had been studying Sam's reaction to all this new information. Now, to Sam's relief, she took control of the conversation and redirected it back to their reason for being here. "I didn't realize you had a family. We'll do our best to keep the disruption to a minimum."

"Please, I don't want you to worry about that. I work at home but I'll…we'll stay out of your way."

The questions kept tumbling through Sam's mind. Had his wife left him? No surprise there, but to leave her child behind? How could she? Then again, based on her experience with the Harris family, she might not have had any say in the matter. AJ working at home was a surprise, though. He was in line to take over the business when his father retired. Could he run such a huge company from home?

Sam realized she was still staring at him while he continued to avoid looking at her. He'd never worn a ring, but that didn't mean he wasn't married when they were dating. *Who are you kidding?* They had never gone on a date. All they did was sleep together. After his father's ultimatum, she had assumed AJ kept their affair a secret because, like his father, he'd thought she was good enough to sleep with a Harris but not good enough to *be* a Harris. Now it seemed he wasn't just arrogant, he was married. Ringless, but married.

"Sam?" Claire's voice gently interrupted her nightmarish journey through the past. "What are your thoughts about the kitchen?"

They could throw a stick of dynamite in it for all she cared. "We should paint the cabinets, for sure. Replace the counter and flooring, and bring in another new light fixture." She should take a closer look at the sink and faucet, but she would have to cross the kitchen to do that. Then she'd be standing by the window and…and she couldn't look out there. Not yet. She needed time to adjust to the reality that AJ had a son…and she didn't.

Three years ago she'd given away a part of herself when she'd put her son up for adoption. She hadn't even had the luxury of mourning her loss. She'd had to get back to work because she had to put food on the table, pay rent and her mother's medical bills. She had coped with her loss the same way she coped with everything else in her life—by carrying on with her responsibilities and not letting herself think about how much her life sucked.

But this…finding out that he'd been able to keep his son while she'd had to give up hers…this felt like more than she could handle. Oh, God. Now she was having trouble breathing again. She glanced over her shoulder toward the front of the house. Maybe she should make an excuse to leave. She could tell Kristi and Claire that she had to get home to her mother, that they could continue with the site visit and fill her in tomorrow.

AJ spoke first. "I have work to do so unless you need me for anything, I'll let the three of you get to it."

Claire, the consummate professional, was quick to respond. "Of course. Please don't let us keep you. This should only take an hour, maybe less. We can let ourselves out and I'll call you tomorrow, after we've worked out our expenses and a timeline for getting everything done."

He responded with a nod and a vague smile and left the kitchen. Sam could tell he was deliberately ignoring her. She wanted to throw her tape measure at him.

She had good aim and she could easily hit him squarely in the back of the head. Seconds later the slam of an outside door was followed by the sound of his footsteps on stairs. Whatever work he had to do, it was in the backyard. With his son.

Claire faced Sam, one hand clutching her iPad, the other on her hip. "What on earth was that all about?"

Tears tickled Sam's eyelids. *You will not cry,* she told herself. *Not here. He's* not *worth it.* "What do you mean?" she asked, trying to feign surprise, knowing she failed miserably. Trust Claire to figure this out.

"Don't give me that. It's totally obvious you and the man in black have a past, and it clearly didn't end well."

That was the understatement of the century. Sam shook her head. "I can't talk about it here. I'll fill you in later."

Claire hugged her. "Sorry, hon. I had no idea."

Kristi made it a group hug. "Will you be able to handle this?"

Sam momentarily indulged in her friends' affection, then pulled away and put on a brave face. "I'll be fine. And there's no way you could have known. If I paid more attention to who our clients are, I wouldn't have been blindsided."

Claire wasn't letting go that easily. "We're almost into December and the pre-Christmas season is always slow. This is a big job and we can really use the business right now, but if—"

Sam took a deep breath and a step back. "No 'buts.' We're taking this job. I'll be fine. It's just…I didn't expect this to be his house and seeing him caught me off guard, but I'll be fine." She had to be. The company might need the work, but she needed the income even more. "Can we finish up and get out of here?"

"Of course. Let's check out the rest of the main floor," Claire said. "There's a big living room, plus the dining room and a small den. Then we can do the upstairs."

Sam's heart started to race again. The bedrooms would be upstairs. AJ's bedroom. Had he and his wife lived here? Had he and his son moved in after they split up? It didn't matter. He lived here now, and his bedroom had better not need any work. There could be a gaping hole in the ceiling, and it would stay that way because it would be a frosty day in hell before she would set a foot in AJ's bedroom.

HALF AN HOUR LATER SAM stood with Claire and Kristi in the upstairs hallway, staring into the bathroom. It had been renovated in the fifties, complete with pink lino on the floor and pink and black ceramic tiles on the walls.

Kristi laughed. "This is one of the tackiest bathrooms I've ever seen. What were they thinking? Thank goodness the fixtures are white. That'll keep the cost down if we decide to renovate."

Sam thought about the bathroom in the apartment she shared with her mother. It had crumbling grout and no personality, but, oddly enough, she liked this one. Her mother would, too.

Claire stepped into the room. "I'm not sure we should. Bathroom renos are time-consuming and expensive. Leaving this as is would mean more money in the client's pocket, and this retro look is surprisingly popular." She picked up a pink crocheted doll covering a roll of toilet paper. "But, oh, my goodness, I've never seen a house with so much stuff in it. Bad enough there's a ton of these kinds of things." She set the doll down and picked up a matching tissue-box holder. "And seriously, how many doilies does one person need?"

Kristi laughed. "I counted eighty-seven on the main floor before I lost track. On the plus side, if the client is interested in getting rid of the vintage linens, most will fetch a few dollars apiece."

Sam couldn't imagine AJ having an attachment to his grandmother's fussy clutter. And Kristi might be right about the linens, but no one would want kitschy crocheted bathroom accessories.

"Sam? What are your thoughts?" Claire asked.

She didn't much care whether AJ saved any money, but she was completely on board with saving time. "I say we leave it. After Kristi works her magic in here, it'll look great."

Claire was making notes as she left the bathroom. "Good plan. Let's check out the bedrooms."

"How can you walk, talk and type at the same time?" Kristi asked.

Claire grinned. "What can I say? It's a gift."

Sam had always admired her business partner's multitasking abilities, and she had never been more grateful for Claire's levelheaded business savvy than she was right now because she knew she could count on her to keep her grounded through this ordeal. Kristi was, well, not so grounded. She tended to leap before she looked and talk before she thought, rushed into everything with boundless enthusiasm, and everyone loved her for it. Or in spite of it. But Kristi would have her back, too. Together they'd get through this, and then Sam's life could get back to normal. Not that she had a "normal" life, but there was a lot to be said for maintaining the status quo.

"Let's check out the bedrooms," Claire said. "This

looks like the master, and I'm guessing it was the grand-mother's."

Kristi groaned. "More doilies and plastic flower ar-rangements. Those must go with the bowl of plastic fruit on the dining-room table."

Sam looked past the clutter to the flower-and-butterfly-patterned wallpaper. "After everything's cleared out, I'll need a day to strip the wallpaper and another day to paint. The oak floor is in good shape, though."

Claire made more notes on the move. "This must be AJ's room." She shot a quick glance at Sam.

Sam hastily perused the room from the doorway and stepped back. The space was neat as a pin, almost austere compared to the grandmother's, and even better there was no wallpaper.

"From too much personality in Grandma's room to none in here," Kristi said. "I get that he's a guy, and guys usually don't have a clue when it comes to deco-rating, but this room is so boring it's painful. Doesn't need much work, though. A fresh coat of paint and some new drapes should do it."

The room had better be able to paint itself, Sam thought, because she wasn't doing it. The simple fact that it was *his* room was enough to get her heart pound-ing, but what if he and his wife had lived here? Con-ceived their child in this bed?

"Two more rooms," Claire said. "This must be the nanny's."

Sam took one look and fell in love with it. The nan-ny's room was hands down the most welcoming space in the house. Although it was a typically gray late-November day in Seattle, the room felt bright, almost sunny. Strangely so, Sam thought. Right now the only occupant was a teddy bear snuggled into the corner of an overstuffed yellow upholstered armchair with a copy of *Green Eggs and Ham* on the seat next to him. Sam could practically hear the warm laughter that would accompany story time. On the floor next to the chair sat a basket full of colorful yarn and knitting needles, and adjacent to that a small round side table painted bright blue. On top of the table there was a vase filled with fresh-cut flowers and a quirky-looking tea service on a wooden tray, a teapot in the shape of a giant strawberry and two pink china cups and saucers. Tea for two. *The nanny and AJ's son?* Sam wondered.

Claire walked into the room and admired the china. "This is so adorable. I've never seen heart-shaped saucers."

Sam's heart felt as flat as a pancake, as though the life was being squeezed out of it. She had never been entertained with tea parties, not even as a very young child. Even back then her mother hadn't been well and although her father had dutifully provided the basics, there'd been no fun, no games, no laughter. But this woman, the nanny, had moved in here and created a personal space that both fit with the rest of the house and was yet set apart from it, and its welcome hominess gave Sam a good feeling about her.

"This room is perfect," Kristi said. "Even the wallpaper works in here. I wouldn't change a thing."

Neither would Sam.

"Excellent." Claire made a note of that. "That leaves the nursery, which is right here across the hall. Should we take a look?"

Sam nodded a silent affirmative, and cast one last look at the nanny's room before reluctantly following her partners to the room across the hall. Earlier when they'd been in the kitchen, she had deliberately avoided looking outside because she was emotionally unprepared to see AJ's son. And now she wasn't ready for this.

The nursery, the only room in the house with a bright modern flair, had been painted a fresh shade of pale green. The child-size trundle bed was covered with a cozy patchwork quilt and heaped with stuffed animals. The green-and-yellow polka-dot upholstery on the armchair and ottoman coordinated with the multitoned green-and-yellow-striped drapes on the window next to them. Had AJ chosen these colors, this furniture? Did he sit here with his son? She didn't know why, but she found it impossible to picture him as a father. Or had his wife decorated the room before she left? Did she still visit? Did the child live with her part of the time?

"Sam?" Claire's gentle tone eased her out of her daze. "I was saying the bedrooms shouldn't take long, since the nanny's room and nursery are fine as they are."

"Sorry, and yes, you're right. The other two bedrooms won't take long. I guess we should start with the grandmother's since no one's living in it. I'll have to move the furniture away from the walls to get at the wallpaper."

"You'll need help with that," Claire said. "I'll get Marlie to call the movers as soon as I get back to the office this afternoon and find out when they're available. We'll have them do the room when they rearrange things downstairs."

Kristi stowed her camera in her shoulder bag. "I'm going home to download the photographs I took today and spend the afternoon working on a color scheme. I want to be home when Jenna gets out of school because yesterday my sweet darling daughter had a *boy* there when I got home."

"Ah, the teenage years," Claire said with a grin. "I remember them well. Except I didn't have a boyfriend," she added quickly.

Neither did Sam. She'd never invited a friend home, either, and wouldn't have dreamed of bringing home a boy she was interested in. He would have made a run for it.

"I remember those years, too." Kristi sighed. "I also remember what teenage boys are like. Hormones permanently in overdrive. That's kind of how I got to be a mom so young."

"You were eighteen when your daughter was born," Sam said because she felt she should say something reassuring. "Jenna's only thirteen."

Kristi rolled her eyes. "Thirteen going on twenty-something."

"And the boy?" Claire asked.

"She says he's fifteen, which, knowing my daughter, means he's probably closer to sixteen."

Claire put an arm around Kristi. "Young girls always date up. Besides, Jenna's a good kid with a good head on her shoulders. I'd give a lot to have one just like her."

From the time the three of them had become business partners, Claire had talked about how desperately she wanted children. Now that her marriage was on the rocks, the likelihood of that was slimmer than ever. Sam didn't allow herself to think about a family, or the future. It was too hard. Hell, just seeing another little boy's bedroom had sent her mind racing back into the past.

What if…?

If only…

Don't go there!

"Do you have plans for the rest of the day, Sam?"

She gave herself another mental shake. "Ah, yes. Stop at the drugstore to pick up my mother's medication. Grab a few groceries." Precious few after she paid for the prescription.

"How is she?" Kristi asked. "Any better?"

Sam wished she hadn't said anything. Although Claire and Kristi had never met her mother, she had reluctantly told them about her. There were days when Sam couldn't leave her alone, and her business partners needed to know why.

She shrugged. "A little better, I think." She hoped, but she didn't want to talk about her mother. "After dinner I'll go over my notes and come up with a time-line for getting all this work done. I'll email it to both of you and we can go over it at our meeting tomorrow morning."

"Excellent," Claire said. "I'll do two appraisals—one for the house as it is now and another that will include all the proposed updates. We can present the package to…the client." She eyed Sam over the top rim of her dark-framed glasses. "Then we'll take it from there."

The three of them trooped down the back stairs to the kitchen, Sam last and desperately hoping to avoid another encounter with "the client." In the kitchen they were greeted by an aproned silver-haired woman, who stood at the stove stirring a large pot. The savory-scented steam rising from it reminded Sam's stomach it was almost lunchtime.

"Hello, girls. I'm Annie Dobson, the nanny."

"Nice to meet you." Claire shook the woman's hand and stepped back. "What are you cooking? It smells wonderful."

"Homemade chicken noodle soup. It's a favorite around here."

Sam's stomach rumbled hungrily.

"We'll get out of your way so you can have lunch," Claire said. "Is Mr. Harris…I mean, is AJ around?"

"He had to go out, so he took young William with him. Would you like me to pass along a message?"

So, his son's name was William.

"Yes, that would be great. Please let him know I'll call as soon as we have a work plan in place. I'm Claire, by the way. This is Kristi, the interior decorator, and Sam's our carpenter."

"Nice to meet you. It'll be nice having some young women around here for a change, especially a lady carpenter." Her blue-eyed gaze gave Sam a good going-over. "You look familiar. Have we met before?"

"Um…" Sam searched her memory for an image of the woman. Had she worked for the Harris family when Sam had renovated their corporate offices? She was a nanny, so unlikely. "No, I don't think so."

Annie's scrutiny didn't let up. "No, maybe not. I usually never forget a face, though, and there's something about you…" She looked away finally and gave the pot of soup another stir. "I'm sure it'll come to me. Oh, I almost forgot. Mr. Harris asked me to give each of you a key to the front door so you can come and go as you please." She pulled the keys out of her apron pocket.

"Thanks." Claire accepted the keys and passed them around.

Sam tucked hers in the pocket of her jeans. "Nice to meet you. I should go," she said to Claire and Kristi. "I have lots to do." And she wanted to get out of here before AJ returned. She still had a lot of questions, like did he plan to live here while they did the work or would he make other arrangements? His parents' home on Mercer Island was certainly big enough. The apartment Sam shared with her mother would fit in their pool house, with room to spare.

Sam hated giving a rat's ass about his living arrangements, hated herself for hoping he'd be here every day and hated that she still found him the most attractive man she had ever met.

Chapter Three

After a nearly sleepless night spent contemplating his options, AJ decided to honor the contract with Sam's company. Getting out of it would take time, and money. Hiring someone else to do the work would take more time. There was also a chance that firing them would raise Sam's suspicions, and he couldn't risk that.

Not that it should matter. She had abruptly and cold-heartedly ended their relationship, neglected to tell him she was pregnant and then decided to put their baby up for adoption as though he had no say in the matter. It was purely by coincidence that, months after Sam had broken things off with him, he happened to see her. He'd been sitting in the glass-walled boardroom of the law firm that handled Harris Marketing and Communications' contract negotiations and had been stunned to see Sam Elliott—*a very pregnant Sam Elliott*—walk out of Melanie Morrow's office. Melanie practiced family law. AJ had met her at a handful of social gatherings and didn't know her well, but well enough to know she wanted to get ahead and make a name for herself, mostly by handling high-profile divorce cases.

He'd never had much interest in contracts—he much preferred the creative side of the business—but his father had insisted he take an active role. That day he had suffered through the meeting and while the lawyers argued about costs and compensations, he had pondered Sam's protruding belly, performed some mental calculations of his own and quickly came to the conclusion that what was inside that belly could very well be his. Was it possible that the woman he had been so in love with could be carrying his child without telling him? It was impossible to believe she was that coldhearted, and having another man's baby would certainly explain why she'd given AJ the brush-off. And now she and that other man were already headed for a divorce, or so it would seem. If that was the case, it was none of his business, but he needed to know.

By the time the meeting was over, he'd come up with a plan to stop by Melanie's office on his way out, invite her to join him for a drink after work and figure out a way to direct the conversation around to Sam. He'd never been much for small talk but that hadn't mattered because two wine spritzers had been all it took to loosen Melanie's tongue.

What he learned was something he'd never imagined possible, and it hit him harder than anything up until then, even harder than his brother's suicide all those years ago. Sam wasn't married. Her baby was due in two months, the father wasn't "involved," she didn't want the baby and she was setting up a private adoption. Counting back from her due date showed the baby had been conceived when they were together. He wasn't sure what he thought of Sam at that moment, but he was absolutely sure of two things. She didn't sleep around, and she was having his baby. A baby she didn't want. The realization cut him to the core. It had taken a week to come up with a plan, then he'd asked Melanie out for dinner, and the rest was history.

A history that yesterday had crashed into his life like a steamroller. He had always intended to get away from Seattle before this could happen. Now that it had, and as bizarre as it sounded even in his head, keeping Sam around to do the work was safer than sending her packing. Claire DeAngelo, who seemed to be the one in charge although she insisted the three of them were equal partners, thought the work would take several weeks and she'd have the house on the market before Christmas.

He'd been up since before dawn, moving everything from the sunroom he used as an office to his bedroom. Satisfied that his temporary work space would provide a welcome escape from the past and present, he went downstairs to join Will and Annie for breakfast and wait for Sam's return.

AFTER AN EARLY-MORNING run, Sam dawdled over her cornflakes and coffee while she watched her mother study the jigsaw puzzle pieces strewn across the other side of the table. For the first time in forever, she was tempted to join her. The notion of withdrawing from reality and into her mother's fantasy world had never held any appeal—until this morning. There'd be no puzzles in Sam's dreamworld. It would also be a world devoid of lying, cheating, two-timing ex-lovers.

In spite of the psychiatrist's diagnosis, years ago, that Tildy Elliott had an illness, a mental illness, Sam had always wondered if some past event had caused her to retreat into a fantasy world. Maybe something Sam's long-absent and now deceased father had done, or something another man had done. Until her run-in with AJ yesterday, Sam had never thought of it in exactly those terms, but now as she watched this delicate woman intent on finding the puzzle's flat-edged border pieces, Sam had a hunch that a man had to be behind her mother's illness. Men were nothing but trouble.

On the weekend, Tildy had been as delighted as a child on Christmas morning when Sam brought the six new puzzles home. This one—a photograph of a castle somewhere in Europe—had immediately captured her mother's interest. It also had a thousand pieces and would easily keep her busy all day while Sam was at work.

Sam dismissed the guilt pangs. When she wasn't working, which was rare these days, she tried to get her mother out of the apartment or at least encourage her to do something other than puzzles, playing solitaire or watching television. But when she had to leave her here alone, she worried less knowing she was occupied, and she knew Tildy would work tirelessly on the puzzle until it was finished.

This morning Sam's very existence felt a lot like those scattered bits of cardboard. Broken pieces of what had been, until yesterday, a whole picture, albeit a tenuous one. Much as she disliked puzzles, she would give almost anything to stay here and lose herself in the mind-numbing activity of putting that picture back together. Instead she had demons to face, and AJ Harris was one hell of a demon.

He'd inherited an incredible house but it needed a lot of work. Still, if she worked long hours and brought in a couple of assistants to help with the painting and wallpaper removal, she should be able to finish in three weeks. Barring any unforeseen problems. To her question about potential problems like mold or termites or faulty wiring, AJ had given one of his silent shrugs. Huh. The privileged pretty boy with the perfect home and an adorably cherub-faced, at least according to Kristi, little boy knew nothing about construction. No surprise there.

There might have been a time when she could have forgiven him for getting his father to do his dirty work, but knowing he'd then gone ahead and had a child with another woman while she'd had to give up hers? *That* was unforgivable. That was the agony she'd have to endure every day for the next three weeks. To make matters worse, he worked at home now. Somehow she would have to guard against drowning in the depths of his dark, soulless gaze. Keep her heart from hammering its way out of her chest every time she watched him cross a room, because to save her sanity she couldn't stop picturing his magnificent male form, completely unclothed.

She jumped up from the table. *Do* not *think of him naked. AJ Harris is* not *the most heart-stoppingly handsome man in the universe. He's the arrogant jerk who ruined your life.* An arrogant, *adulterous* jerk who'd been screwing her while he'd been busy getting his wife pregnant. Well, to hell with him. Sam had coped with a lot of crap in her life, and she would find a way to cope with this, too.

She gathered up the breakfast dishes. The soggy remains of her mother's cereal went down the drain— she'd eaten a few mouthfuls, at least—and then Sam quickly washed her breakfast dishes and put them in the drain rack on the counter. Her mother's head was still bent over the puzzle pieces. "More coffee, Mom?"

"No, thank you, dear." She snapped another puzzle

piece into place. "Look at this. The top edge and one side are almost done."

Sam dried her hands on a towel and hung it on the handle of the oven door. "I see that. You're doing great."

"It's always best to start with the outside edges and work your way in."

While Sam pondered that as a possible metaphor for her life, she packed two bottles of water, a sandwich and an apple in her insulated lunch bag. "I left some tuna salad in the fridge for you, and Mrs. Stanton said she'd drop by to see you at lunchtime." Mrs. Stanton was the neighbor across the hall. Years ago Sam had given the woman a key so she could come in at lunchtime to make sure Tildy had something to eat. Sam so often dreamed of moving into a decent apartment, maybe even a house with a back garden that might tempt her mother out of her reclusive existence, but what if the upheaval was the tipping point for Tildy's fragile mental state? That worried her, and more important, there'd be no Mrs. Stanton to keep an eye on her.

Sam retrieved her work boots from the tiny hall closet, slipped into her jacket and picked up her clipboard from the hall table. "I'm leaving for work, Mom. Do you need to do anything before I leave?"

"Oh. I'm afraid we're out of milk. The queen is coming this afternoon and she likes milk in her tea. Not cream. It has to be milk, you know."

Sam sighed and returned to the kitchen. "I bought milk yesterday." She opened the refrigerator. "It's right here, see?"

Tildy's glossy red lips spread into a smile. "Oh, thank you, dear. The last time she came, she caused a royal fuss because there was only cream."

Sam *never* bought cream, but that was the thing

about fictional events. A person's memories could be anything she wanted them to be.

"She liked the cucumber sandwiches, though. And I'm out of cigarettes. Could you pick some up for me on your way home?"

"Sure." *As soon as hell freezes over.* Her mother had been out of cigarettes for fifteen years. Sam had stopped buying them after her father left because they couldn't afford them, she was tired of smelling like an ashtray and she worried her mother would set the place on fire. From time to time Tildy still asked for them and it was simpler to say yes than to remind her that she didn't smoke anymore.

Sam slipped an arm around her mother's narrow shoulders and gave them a gentle squeeze. This morning she was still wearing her chartreuse satin dressing gown but as always she had teased her thinning silver hair into a poofy do and rouged her cheeks to match her lips. The tang of hair spray that shellacked her mother's hair in place made Sam back away. "What are you doing today?" she asked. *Aside from entertaining Her Majesty.* "Any plans?"

"I'll finish the puzzle." She turned her attention back to the jigsaw pieces spread across the kitchen table's worn Arborite. "And then I have to get ready for tea. I've decided to wear the green-and-gold plaid silk. You don't think it's too flashy, do you?"

Not if the queen is color-blind. The dress her mother referred to wear was every bit as hideous now as it had been forty years ago. "Everyone loves your plaid dress, Mom. You'll look beautiful," Sam lied, carefully sidestepping any mention of Elizabeth II.

"Yes, I'm hoping she'll like it, too," Tildy said. "It's in terribly bad taste to upstage the queen."

Of course it was.

Her mother's delusions were richly populated with royalty and Hollywood stars, and occasional appearances by the Pope. Sam could almost understand her mother's preoccupation with the likes of Robert De Niro and Steve Martin, even the British monarchy, but the significance of those papal visits eluded her. Her mother wasn't even Catholic, although she could almost pass for pious in the habit she'd fashioned from an old black robe, a dingy white pillowcase and a rosary of pink plastic beads.

"I'll see you tonight, Mom. If I'm late, Mrs. Stanton will drop by again."

"That's nice." Tildy straightened then and stared down at Sam's feet. "Why are you galumphing around my kitchen in those boots?"

"I'm going to work, remember?"

"Will you be back in time for tea?"

"Sorry. Not today."

First thing, she had a meeting with Claire and Kristi, then she had to stop at the building supply store. The rest of the day would be spent avoiding AJ while she stripped wallpaper and patched the walls, and Kristi cleared countless decades' worth of clutter out of the kitchen. If all went well, Sam would be home in time to fix dinner. If not, she'd have to call Mrs. Stanton and ask her to take Tildy a plate of whatever she and Mr. Stanton were having tonight. Her mother barely ate enough to keep a bird alive, and although Sam wrote her neighbor a check for a hundred dollars every month to cover the cost of food, she hated asking for favors. On the plus side, her mother had never shown any inclination to cook for herself, so at least no one had to worry about her starting a fire in the kitchen.

"See you tonight, Mom."

Tildy snapped another puzzle piece into place.

"I love you." Sam always said it, but her mother never reciprocated. No one ever had. Not her father. Certainly not AJ, and yesterday she'd discovered why. He hadn't loved her. He'd been married to someone else.

Today was no different. "Don't forget to buy milk," Tildy said without looking up.

Sam didn't reply, she just sighed as she let herself out of the apartment, locked the door and knocked on the one across the hall.

"Good morning, Sam," Elizabeth Stanton said when she opened the door. She was a tall, boney-looking woman, fiftyish with salt-and-pepper hair, married to a man fifteen years her senior. "How's everything this morning?"

"Same as usual. Mom's working on a puzzle right now. I left some tuna salad in the fridge and bread to make a sandwich, if you can get her to eat one."

"She usually will, as long as I cut the crusts off. I've got some leftover pumpkin pie from Thanksgiving so I'll take her a slice of that, too."

"If she calls to tell you we're out of milk, just tell her you'll bring some over at lunchtime. There's plenty in the fridge, but she keeps forgetting about it."

Mrs. Stanton displayed a prominent overbite when she smiled. "I take it she's having tea this afternoon?"

"I'm afraid so."

"It's harmless," the woman said. "You should count your blessings for that because you can't say the same for everyone who has her condition."

"You're right." She had trouble seeing it as a blessing, but as curses went, it could have been a lot worse.

"I've been hoping the new medication will make a difference."

"I am, too, especially for your sake, but you need to give it some time."

"I know." That's what the doctor had said, too. "I'm starting a new job today but I'll try to be home in time for dinner."

"Have a good day, Sam. Let me know if you'll be late and I'll run across with some dinner for her, too."

She closed the door, and Sam trudged down the hallway to the stairwell, leaving one set of problems behind and setting off to face another.

WILL SCOOPED A FORKFUL of his eggs off his plate as AJ walked into the kitchen. "Daddy, I eating green eggs an' ham. See?" He held up the food, then popped it into his mouth.

"I see that. It looks delicious."

After Will had fallen in love with the Dr. Seuss story, Annie had cleverly concocted a recipe for scrambled eggs with chopped ham and spinach. "Good way to get some greens into him," she'd said, and as usual she was right. Will loved it, and AJ had to admit he did, too. He poured himself a cup of coffee and sat next to his son with his own plate of green eggs and ham.

"Will you be working today, Mr. Harris?"

He unfolded the morning paper and scanned the headlines. "This afternoon I will be—the gardening article I'm working on is due tomorrow—but I'll take Will and Hershey to the park this morning."

"Good idea. It's supposed to rain this afternoon. Did those women say what time they'd be here?"

"Around ten-thirty. Claire DeAngelo called last night to say they had a meeting first thing, but they'd be here after that." He intended to be out of the house by then. "The interior decorator, I think her name is Kristi, would like to start clearing out the kitchen. I hope you don't mind."

"Not at all. I plan to do a little Christmas baking before they arrive, then I can give her a hand."

"Thanks. If there's anything you'd like to keep, I want you to feel free."

"That's very generous of you. I'm mighty fond of a couple of your grandmother's teapots."

"Then I want you to have them." It wasn't as though there was any shortage of teapots in this house.

Will's fork clattered to the table. "Going to park now?" he mumbled around his last mouthful of eggs.

"Remember your manners, William," Annie said. "Good little boys don't talk with their mouths full, do they?"

Will swallowed. "All gone." To demonstrate, he opened his mouth wide.

Annie laughed and lifted him down from the table. "Come with me. We'll wash your hands and face and get your jacket and mittens while your father finishes his breakfast."

AJ watched them leave the kitchen, admiring her patience. He should be taking notes because it wouldn't be long before he would be taking care of William on his own. He looked forward to it, but that didn't mean he didn't have regrets.

Adopting his own son hadn't been the first time he'd used the family fortune and status to get something he wanted, but it would be the last. His parents, make that his father, had issued an ultimatum the day he'd brought William home. He could keep his position in the business or he could keep his illegitimate son. One or the other. Not both.

His decision had been a no-brainer and he'd never regretted putting his son first. Grandmother Harris, horrified by her son's hard-hearted stand, had opened her door to AJ and William. Her health was failing and he couldn't turn his back on her, so although he had already purchased the house in Idaho, he'd moved in with his son and hired Annie Dobson to look after them. His grandmother was able to spend her final years getting to know her great-grandson in the home she loved. AJ had never regretted doing what he'd had to do to get his son, and he never would. He hadn't regretted postponing the move to Idaho, either. Now, as long as he was careful, he wouldn't regret letting Sam's company sell this house. He hoped.

Chapter Four

Ready Set Sold's downtown office was already open when Sam arrived, and Marlie, their office manager, was talking into her headset. Six months after opening the business they had advertised for an office manager and the decision to hire Marlie had been unanimous. Her name was short for Marline. She'd had impeccable references, a no-nonsense approach to dealing with clients, big hair and an even bigger heart. She referred to Sam, Kristi and Claire as "Marlie's angels," and they loved it.

Marlie's wardrobe consisted of pencil skirts and matching stilettos in every color under the sun, and snug-fitting sweaters that made the most, and then some, of her generous proportions. In spite of the artificial nails, always painted to match her outfit, she could type like the wind. Today's nail color was pistachio but the sweater was turquoise, which meant the polish probably went with the skirt. Sam couldn't see it from where she was standing. Marlie greeted Sam with a shiny green-tipped finger wave and indicated she'd be off the phone in a minute, maybe two.

Sam slid two envelopes filled with receipts from under the clip on her clipboard and tossed them into the in-box on Marlie's desk. Then she stepped into the tiny office.

Their office, on the second floor of an old building near Pioneer Square, consisted of a small reception area that served as Marlie's domain and an even smaller office shared by the three business partners. Sam ran the construction end of the business out of her dilapidated old delivery-truck-slash-mobile-workshop she'd had since she worked on her own, and Kristi managed her design and home staging service out of her mommy-and-me minivan.

Claire used the office more than either Sam or Kristi did—often to meet with clients—and the space mostly reflected her style. She had arranged the stapler, tape dispenser and pencil holder on the sleek, dark espresso-colored desk with the same precision she did everything, which told Sam she'd been the last one to use the space. Kristi's style was anything but exact. She liked to group unlikely things together and when she did, they were arranged for effect, not accuracy. On the rare occasions when Sam worked in here, she always put everything back the way she found it, regardless who had put it there.

Against the back wall behind the desk was a matching credenza, and above it hung three framed photographs of recent projects. This display was Kristi's contribution and she changed the photos every month. In the current display was the house in Beacon Hill with Claire's sold sign in the front yard, a before-and-after collage of a bathroom reno Sam had done in a house in Washington Park and one of Kristi's clutter crew at work on an elderly woman's Bellevue condominium.

Sam sighed. Next month the display would almost certainly include a photograph of AJ's house—yet another reminder he'd made another brief, unwelcome appearance in her life. At least by then the house would be finished and he would be out of her life, again, this time forever.

Sam set her clipboard on the desk and scanned the schedule on the whiteboard while she shrugged out of her jacket and hooked it on the coat tree in the corner. Claire had obviously been here after they toured AJ's house yesterday afternoon because the rough schedule they'd come up with during the inspection had already been added.

"G'morning, Sam." An hourglass Marlie stood in the doorway, barely five foot five in spite of her spike-heeled shoes. "Did you get your messages?"

"Not yet. Anything important?"

"Darlin', it's all important. The movers called about fifteen minutes ago to say they've already emptied out the foyer at the Harris house. The building supply store called to say they'll deliver the Hendricks' new kitchen countertop by the end of the week. And…" She shuffled the message slips in her hand. "Oh, your mom called."

Of course she had. She'd probably called Mrs. Stanton as well, and when Sam got back to her truck where she'd forgotten her phone, she'd probably find a message from her, too.

Marlie glanced up from her notepad. "She wants you to pick up milk on your way home."

Sam sighed.

Marlie laughed. "Let me guess. You're not out of milk."

"We're not. She's having tea with…she's having tea this afternoon and she probably didn't think to check the fridge before she called."

Instead of asking for more details, Marlie gave her a sympathetic hug. "How is she these days?"

"No change so far. The doctor said it could take several weeks before we'll know if the new medication will make a difference." Providing there'd be a difference. The doctor had warned there was no guarantee, but given how outrageously expensive these new meds were, Sam sincerely hoped there would be.

"You're a good girl," Marlie said. "It takes a special person to do what you do."

"She's my mom. I'd do anything for her." Which was true, and she really did love her mother in spite of the almost-daily challenges. There were days, though, when she secretly wished their relationship was less of a dead-end one-way alley and more like a two-way street. Like today. Today it would have felt good to hear someone say "I love you, too."

Marlie patted her arm and returned to the reception area. "I see you dropped off your receipts for the work on the Matheson house. Is this it or will you have more expenses?"

"No, I'm finished and Kristi should be, too. It's in Claire's hands now."

As if on cue, the door flew open and Claire breezed in, quirking an eyebrow to indicate she'd heard her name. *Good morning,* she mouthed. With her briefcase slung over one shoulder and her Bluetooth in her ear, carrying on a one-sided conversation, she moved purposefully through reception and into the office and, in one fluid motion, slid her bag onto the desk, took out her iPad and started keying in information. The woman had more multitasking skills in her baby finger than all of Sam and Kristi put together.

"That's two angels accounted for," Marlie said,

glancing at her glittery gold bangle wristwatch. "I wonder what'll hold Kristi up this morning." She said it with affection, not criticism.

Any number of things could delay Kristi. Her daughter, Jenna, couldn't find her homework. The dog had barfed on the carpet. The minivan was out of gas. Kristi could march into the most cluttered and disorganized home and have it shipshape in no time. Her own life was a different story, though, and Sam suspected she thrived on the chaos.

Sam retrieved her clipboard and jacket and perched on the corner of Marlie's desk, checking her notes and to-do list while she waited for Claire to wrap up her phone call.

She had already checked her notes at least three times this morning and was sure she hadn't missed anything. They'd come up with a three-week timeline for this project and she wanted to finish by then, if not sooner. No surprises.

"You look like you've been to the gym," Sam said when Claire emerged from the office.

Claire shook her head without taking her eyes off the screen of her iPad. Her dark shoulder-length hair had been swept back into a ponytail and she was wearing slim-fitting black exercise pants and a bright yellow tank top. "Not yet. I don't have any appointments this morning, though, so I'll go right after our meeting. Want to come with? I have a couple of guest passes."

"Tempting, but I have to get to work as soon as our meeting's over." Too bad, because the only way she could afford to set foot in Claire's gym was as a guest. "I went for a run first thing this morning, though." She loved to run, especially early in the morning when the city hadn't fully woken from its slumber. After ten minutes or so she got into the zone. With her feet pounding the pavement and her heart pounding in her chest, after her breathing went from ragged to fast and controlled, she would fix her gaze on something in the distance and her only thought was getting there. Then she'd focus on another distant spot, and another, letting her mind go blank while her stride devoured the miles. Eventually her body would tell her when it was time to quit and she had learned to listen, even though it brought her back to reality.

"Good for you. Oh, that reminds me, I signed up for the half marathon next summer. Are you entering?"

"Ah…I hope to, but I'm not sure yet." If she did, she'd run the whole race, but as always it would depend on whether she had time to train for it.

"We should talk Kristi into signing up, too."

Sam tried to imagine Kristi running to the end of the block. No, not going to happen. "First you'll have to convince her to roll up her yoga mat and buy a pair of running shoes."

Claire set her phone down and checked her watch. "Speaking of Kristi, I wonder what's keeping her—"

Marlie waved at them with the backs of both hands. "I have work to do so why don't you two run along down to the coffee shop and get out of my hair." In typical Marlie fashion, it wasn't a question. "I'll call Kristi and tell her to meet you there."

"Good plan." Claire slipped her iPad into her briefcase. "Do you have everything you need?" she asked Sam.

Sam waved her clipboard and nodded. "All set."

The late-November mist shrouding Pioneer Square made it seem even quieter than usual for that time of the morning. Several people in business attire purposefully made their way to their office buildings, a few tourists wandered around, waiting for the shops to open, and a bag lady sat on a bench feeding a gaggle of pigeons.

By the time they reached the coffee shop, Claire had taken another phone call. She nodded and pulled out her wallet when the clerk asked if she wanted her usual. Claire's "usual" was a large mocha and a toasted bagel with cream cheese. "Sorry, can you hold on a moment please?" She pressed the mute button on her Bluetooth. "I'll take a pot of green tea and a slice of banana loaf, as well. For Kristi," she said to Sam. "That way we can get to work as soon as she gets here."

"Sure thing. Large dark roast for you, right?" he asked Sam. "No room for cream?"

"That's me."

"Anything else?" He always asked.

Her answer was always the same. "No, thanks. I've already eaten." She deliberately avoided looking at the pastries in the display case, though. She could buy half a dozen muffins at the grocery store for the cost of one of these.

Claire paid for her order and dropped a generous handful of change into the tip jar. Sam handed the clerk a pair of ones to pay for her coffee and pocketed her change. After paying for her mom's new medication, she was back to pinching pennies. Claire, who still lived in the luxury penthouse condominium she owned with her soon-to-be ex-husband, had always been more comfortably off than either Sam or Kristi. Probably better off than Sam and Kristi put together. And although Kristi complained about her ex's lack of financial support, she wasn't afraid to spend money. Sam preferred to put hers away for a rainy day than spend it on coffee shop pastries.

The young man behind the counter grabbed a tray. "Have a seat. I'll bring everything over when it's ready."

Claire was already seated and had ended her phone call and pulled out her iPad by the time Sam joined her and set her clipboard on the table. "I've gone over my notes from last week's meeting, and I think everything we discussed has been covered." She swiped a neatly manicured finger across the screen to bring up a fresh slate.

The young man arrived with their order.

"Sorry I'm late!" Kristi dashed in, all smiles and flyaway blond hair, lugging an oversize and over-stuffed handbag and an armload of fabric and wallpaper samples. "I was going over the photos I took at the Harris house yesterday and lost track of time." She plunked herself into a chair, dug out her laptop and a bulging leather-bound organizer, rummaged in her bag for something to write with. "There has to be a pen in here somewhere..."

Claire, never without a spare, handed one to her.

"Thank you!" she said, pouring tea into her cup. "Mmm, I needed this. How much do I owe you?"

"My treat. You can get the next one."

"Thanks!" Kristi flipped her organizer open and laid the pen in the crease. "So, what's on today's agenda?"

Claire studied the screen in front of her. "The Matheson place. Where are we at with that?"

"The last thing I had to do was install the shelves in the laundry room," Sam said. "I finished on Friday and I gave all my receipts to Marlie this morning."

"And those shelves were the perfect way to finish off that room." Kristi brought up a photograph on her laptop. "Aren't they great?"

Claire leaned in for a closer look. "Oh, yes! I like

the plants. Nice touch, and so unexpected in a laundry room."

"That's the whole idea," Kristi said. "After people have seen a dozen houses, they'll remember the one with the awesome laundry room."

"Clever. What's in the baskets?"

"I used those to store the detergent and fabric softener."

"You gals are a pair of geniuses." Claire started typing notes to herself. "I'll call the Mathesons this afternoon and set up an appointment for our first open house."

For the next twenty minutes they worked diligently through Claire's list of projects and wrapped up by agreeing on a work plan for AJ's house. Sam sipped her coffee and jotted notes as necessary onto the lists in her clipboard.

"We have a busy week lined up," Kristi said when they were finished. She stuffed her paint chips and portfolio into her bag and picked up her cup. "And now that we've taken care of business we can move on to the good stuff."

Sam knew exactly what she meant. Their meetings adhered to a strict rule—business before chitchat. If she'd been thinking ahead, she could have planned her getaway before the conversation turned personal. Too late now. Kristi and Claire had already shifted their focus to her, and there'd be no escape until she answered their questions.

The waiter stopped at their table. Claire handed her empty plate to him, then put her elbows on the table and propped her chin on her hands. "I've been dying to hear what's up with you and the man in black."

And here we go, Sam thought. *Right on cue.*

"More hot water for your tea?" the waiter asked Kristi.

"Yes, thanks. That'd be great."

He took the pot and disappeared.

Kristi tossed her hair over her shoulders and grinned. "So…you and AJ Harris. What's that all about?"

Sam squirmed. Even being prepared for these questions didn't make answering them any easier. "What do you mean?"

Claire folded her paper napkin into a neat square. "Nice try. There's something going on between you and AJ Harris."

Sam shook her head. "Not anymore."

"But there was. Anyone can see that."

Reluctantly, Sam nodded. "AJ and me…it didn't last long, and was a long time ago. He worked for his father's company then, I'm not sure what he does now."

"He told me he's a freelance writer," Claire said. "That's why he works at home."

"And now he has a family," Kristi said. "When do you think he got married?"

Sam set her coffee on the table. "I assume it was after we broke up." She only wished she was as certain of that as she sounded.

"So, when were the two of you an item?"

A lifetime ago. She shrugged. "I guess about three and a half years ago."

"What happened?"

"I wasn't good enough for the son of the great James Harris."

"According to…?"

"James Harris."

"What a jerk," Kristi said. "It didn't take AJ long to find someone else."

"What do you mean?"

"You saw his little boy yesterday."

"Actually, I didn't." She had deliberately avoided looking at the child in the backyard.

"AJ said he was two," Kristi said. "I'd say he has to be at least two and a half years old, which means...well, we all know what that means."

Sam stared into the bottom of her empty coffee cup and didn't respond. She had spent all night coming up with possible scenarios for when and how AJ had become a parent, and she hadn't liked any of them.

"So you think the guy's a player?" Claire asked. "His family's loaded and men in that position never have trouble finding women, but I don't know, he doesn't seem like the type. Did the two of you ever talk about having kids?"

Sam shook her head. The conversation was heading down a road that was way too close to home for comfort. "We were never that serious. Like I said yesterday, I did some work for his family's business and..."

"And...?" Claire asked.

"And..." Kristi was always prone to exaggeration. "She and AJ mixed a little pleasure with business."

Sam's face heated up.

"That's obvious," Claire said before Sam could respond. "But there's more to it than that. The two of you must have had a connection back then because you sure as heck have one now."

Sam thought so, too. Until James Harris told her otherwise.

"And he's seriously to-die-for," Kristi said. "The two of you look perfect together."

Claire reached for her hand. "And he's even more

intense than our Sam. I don't think I've seen him smile once."

Kristi grinned and took her other hand. "You're right, but I'll bet our Sam knew how to put a smile on his face."

Claire laughed. "I'll bet he's one of those men who always wears black, isn't he?"

"Mmm, like one of those guys in a movie who's waiting for the right woman to come along and save him from his past," Kristi said.

Inwardly, Sam cringed. They didn't know the half of it. "You two seriously need to stop watching movies and get a life."

"All three of us need to get a life," Claire said. "When was the last time one of us went on a date?"

Sam hoped her casual shrug covered the reality that she was squirming on the inside. She hated talking about personal stuff. "We had a thing for a while. I thought maybe it could be serious, but now...now it looks as though he might already have been married."

"And you know for sure he was?"

She was sure about only one thing. "He didn't want to be with me, and his father *really* didn't want him to be with me, so I ended it."

Last night she had lain in bed in the dark and gone over the timeline in her mind, and over it and over it. She'd been hired to renovate the boardroom at Harris Marketing and Communications. Within a week she and AJ were hot and heavy. Two months later, when she finished the job, old Mr. Harris had given her the final check for her work and told her to stop seeing his son. At the beginning of the conversation, she'd believed AJ would stand up for her as soon as he heard what his father had said. By the end of the conversation, she was sure AJ had put his father up to it, so she'd told him they were done.

A month later, she had to face the fact that she was having AJ's baby, alone. Her son was born in December, just before Christmas. In a couple of weeks he'd be three years old.

For AJ to have a son who was already two, maybe even two and a half if Kristi was right, it meant that his wife was already pregnant when Sam's baby was born, which meant she and AJ had been married and planning a family less than a year after his affair with her.

Was it possible he'd met the woman after ending things with Sam? Yes, but given old man Harris's determination to get rid of her, it was unlikely.

"AJ's father hired me to build custom cabinets and install them in the executive offices and the company's boardroom. AJ and I became…friends."

Kristi rolled her eyes and leaned forward, hands propped under her chin. "You mean you hooked up. Did you do it on the boardroom table?"

Sam struggled to remain unruffled and failed.

"Oh, my God, you totally did!" Kristi elbowed Claire. "I *knew* this was going to be interesting."

"So what happened?" Claire asked, sounding sympathetic. "You and AJ were a lot more than friends with benefits. From what I saw yesterday, the two of you were in love."

"For a while, I thought so, too. I was wrong." Sam struggled to keep the bitterness out of her voice.

"The way he looked at you yesterday? There's still something there." Claire was an excellent judge of character, but this time she was wrong. Whatever emotions

AJ had displayed yesterday—guilt, maybe even a little shame—it wasn't love.

"He does *not* have feelings for me," Sam said. "I thought he did, but then he got his father to break things off with me—"

"His father?"

"You're kidding, right?"

I wish, Sam thought. "He said I didn't have the right background, his son could do a lot better and that…" This was always the worst part. "That my mother needed to be in an institution."

Claire and Kristi stared at her, momentarily speechless, something that almost never happened.

"You hear about families like this in movies," Claire said, the first to find her voice. "But to think people actually do these things is unbelievable."

Kristi took Sam's hand and squeezed it. "Oh, sweetie. You poor thing."

Sam couldn't bring herself to tell them she'd never mentioned her mother to AJ, and to this day she still didn't know how he and his father had found out about Tildy.

Claire squeezed Sam's other hand. "You're probably right about AJ being involved with someone else, maybe even married to her. His father didn't want to make it about his son, so he made it about you."

And he'd pretty much hit the mark, Sam thought. Her background was less than stellar. She came from a broken home, and a poor one at that. Instead of going to college, she'd pursued what she loved, working with her hands, building things, and she was good at it.

"Men really are such jerks." That was Kristi's fallback description of practically every man on the planet, except the ones she called deadbeats.

Claire's eyes softened a little. "He's single now."

He was, and in some ways that was the hardest part to accept. He had walked away from Sam and had a child with another woman while she'd had to give up hers. She felt cheated, and cheated on. Getting involved with AJ now was completely out of the question because she would never trust him, and there was no way she could be a mother to someone else's child.

"Believe me, I am *not* going there again," she said. "But if I want to finish stripping the wallpaper out of that foyer today, I have to get started." She stood up, as much to end the conversation as to make her point.

Claire slid all of her electronic devices into her slim briefcase. "The most important thing for us to remember is that he is a client."

And the client was always right. Blah, blah, blah.

"We're all okay with that, right?" She snapped the case closed and glanced pointedly from Kristi to Sam and back to Kristi.

They nodded like a pair of schoolgirls.

"Are you going with her this morning?" Claire asked Kristi.

"I was planning to get there at lunchtime, but if you think I should—"

"I'll be fine," Sam said, shrugging into her jacket. The work on AJ's house would take three weeks. She'd get in, figure out a way to avoid running into him, get out. It was a big house, after all, and he wouldn't want to see her any more than she wanted to see him, so how difficult could this be?

Chapter Five

Sam stood at AJ's front door, finger on the doorbell button. Ringing it yesterday, when she hadn't had a clue who would answer, had been so easy. Now a crazy mix of reluctance and anticipation swirling inside her head made her a little dizzy. She had his house key on her key ring...how ironic was that?...but she couldn't bring herself to use it. Not yet. She would have to get used to letting herself in, but it didn't feel right for her first day on the job. Maybe if Kristi was here, but she was working with another client this morning and wouldn't be here till lunchtime. Or later, knowing Kristi.

"For heaven's sake, ring the bell already." She forced herself to push the button, stood back as the chimes rang and waited.

A minute later, maybe less, footsteps sounded inside and she braced herself for the moment she would once again be face-to-face with AJ. The nanny opened the door.

An overwhelming sense of relief engulfed her, along with the warmth of the woman's smile and the oven-fresh scent of something sweet and spicy. Cookies? Sam's mouth started to water.

The woman's blue eyes sparkled the way they had the

first time they'd met. Once again Sam had the feeling that life was good for Annie Dobson, and her mission in life was to share the goodness with the rest of the world.

"Good morning, Samantha. Lovely to see you again, dear. Mr. Harris said you'd be here first thing. Is Kristi with you?" She spoke their names as though they'd been lifelong friends instead of strangers who'd only just met.

"Hi. Nice to see you, too, and no, Kristi won't be here till lunchtime."

"Mr. Harris has taken William and the dog out for the morning, but you might as well come on in and get…" Annie's voice trailed off as she took in the equipment Sam had assembled on the veranda. "Oh, my, look at all the things you brought with you."

Sam had already unloaded her toolbox, stepladder, a five-gallon pail of patching compound and the rented wallpaper steamer from her truck. "Tools of the trade," she said. "And I know it looks like a lot, but I always clean up at the end of the day and I'll do my best to keep the mess under control." And although it made no sense, she was a little disappointed AJ wasn't here. *It's just as well he's not,* she reminded herself. With no distractions, she could concentrate on stripping wallpaper. If she could finish this afternoon, she'd be able to patch the plaster walls before she went home and have them sanded and primed by midmorning tomorrow.

Annie beamed at her. "Don't you worry about a thing. You have a job to do, and I have to say it's good to see a woman doing what's usually a man's job. This never happened in my day, but after the three of you left yesterday, I told Mr. Harris having you here will be wonderful for young William. You know, to see a woman like you doing such untraditional work."

Huh. To have been a fly on the wall for that conversation.

"I'm afraid that with the child's mother being out of the picture, there's just me…" Annie's voice trailed off momentarily, then she started up again. "Sorry, dear. I tend to ramble once I get going. You'll get used to me. Would you like some help bringing everything inside?"

Sam reached for her toolbox. "Oh, no, I can manage."

"I'm sure you can manage just fine, dear. You're working here in the foyer today, aren't you? The movers were here first thing and carted that big old hall stand into the living room for the time being. Moved a bunch of other stuff around, including all the furniture in the grandmother's old bedroom. Mr. Harris took everything out of his office this morning and moved it upstairs so he can work there till the main floor is finished."

Sam carefully set her toolbox on the hardwood floor of the foyer, squaring her back toward the sunroom that doubled as AJ's office.

The dinging of a bell from the back of the house caught Annie's attention. "That's the timer. I'm making gingerbread men, thought young William would like to decorate those, what with the holidays coming. You'll let me know if you need anything?"

"Thanks. I will." Sam went back outside to get the rest of her things.

How old was Annie Dobson? she wondered. Somewhere between sixty and a hundred and one, she decided. Ageless, and not so much old as old-fashioned. A cookie-baking granny of a nanny in a pleated wool skirt, with her watch pinned to her sweater and her glasses dangling from a chain around her neck. Sam was completely smitten. Other than a handful of old photographs, she had no memory of her grandmothers, and her own mother had never baked a cookie in her life.

You don't have time to waste feeling sorry for yourself. She forced the emotion out of her mind, but the fantasy life she had created for her son floated into her thoughts. Was his mother baking cookies for him to decorate? Of course she was. And she was planning a cake for his third birthday, and a party, too. Realizing she'd wandered into even more dangerous territory, she plugged in her earphones, cranked the volume on some upbeat music and got to work.

An hour later she had the wallpaper stripped off two walls and decided to clean up the mess she'd made before she tackled the rest.

One minute she was kneeling on the foyer floor, cramming wallpaper into plastic trash bags. The next she was sitting on her butt, getting a serious face-licking from an exuberant brown shaggy-haired dog. Make that a large puppy. And the next she was staring into a pair of soft brown little-boy eyes. She pulled out her earbuds in time to catch his giggles.

"I gots a dog," he said. "Hawshey."

The latter, she guessed, was the dog's name, although she couldn't be sure. She held the dog at bay while its head bobbed from side to side, tongue lapping in an attempt to reconnect with her face. The child put his arms around the dog's neck, and Sam let go. He managed to restrain the squirming mass for a few seconds, then his giggles turned to shrieks as the dog wriggled out of his grasp.

"Will? What are you up to?" AJ strode into the foyer. "Oh."

Sam quickly got to her feet.

"Sorry," he said. "Annie and I will have to do a better job of keeping him and the dog out of your way."

His unexpected appearance rendered Sam speechless. She should say something, but what? *Cute kid. Cute dog. Screw you for having the life that might have been mine.*

The grief swamped her then, as it always did when she let herself dwell on what she'd given up instead of what she'd given her child. The counselor who'd talked to her at the hospital had cautioned her about these feelings, said she would need to remind herself that the personal sacrifice for the sake of her child had been the right thing to do.

"No problem," she said, finally finding her tongue. "They're not in the way."

AJ scanned the bare walls. "The room looks...bigger."

The child's laughter interrupted their stilted conversation. He was trying to wrap the dog in a long, damp strip of flowered-patterned wallpaper. "Look. Hawshey's a present."

"Hershey," AJ said, gently correcting the child's pronunciation.

Ah, Hershey. Like chocolate, Sam thought. *That* made sense.

AJ crouched next to his son and placed his hands on the little boy's shoulders. The gesture seemed more protective than affectionate. "He won't hold still long enough for you to wrap him up like a present. Why don't you take him back to the kitchen? It's almost lunchtime."

William had a mind of his own. "I *like* presents."

"I know you do, but we should see about getting you some lunch."

The child pointed a finger at Sam. "Who's she?"

AJ glanced at her, then quickly looked away. "Her name is Sam."

"Sam-I-am?" William asked. "Sam-I-am, Sam-I-am!"

"It's his favorite story," AJ explained.

Sam had noticed the copy of the Dr. Seuss classic in the nanny's room when she and her partners had toured the house. "Do you like green eggs and ham?" she asked.

The child nodded vigorously. "For breakfast."

"Really? *Green* eggs?"

More nodding.

"Annie makes them," AJ said. "They're good for you, right, Will?"

"Yup." The dog licked the boy's face, making him laugh and wriggle away from his father's grasp, then the pair raced out the room, presumably headed for the kitchen.

Sam watched AJ watch his son disappear. Was it her imagination, or was he a little more relaxed now that the child was gone?

AJ stood up. "She puts spinach in them."

"Excuse me?"

"The eggs. Spinach makes them green."

"Oh. Good idea, I guess." Never, not in a million years, could she have imagined talking to AJ about Dr. Seuss stories and feeding green eggs to a child for breakfast. It must be getting close to lunchtime, though, because even the idea of spinach-green eggs was making her hungry.

AJ glanced around the foyer again, then back to where Sam stood, ankle-deep in wallpaper.

She snagged the garbage bag. "Sorry about the mess. I'll clean this up before I take a lunch break."

"No need to apologize."

She knew that. She was doing what she'd been hired to do, but she didn't know what else to say. He'd come in here to get the boy and the dog. Why hadn't he left with them? Why was he standing here, staring at her as though he still had something to say?

"Is something wrong?" she asked. Few men rattled her the way he did, and none made her feel this alive. Her body ached with physical awareness, to the point where the pleasure bordered on pain.

Her question seemed to catch him off guard. "No. Not at all. I was wondering…" He shrugged. "Wondering how you've been."

That was the best he could come up with? "Isn't it a little late for you to care?" She hadn't intended for it to sound bitchy but she knew it did.

He was unfazed, and he stood his ground. "So that's how it's going to be."

The most important thing for us to remember is that he is a client. Recalling Claire's comment made her regret the snarkiness. "Sorry. That was rude. I've been fine. Getting this business up and running has kept me busy."

He glanced at her hands. "Seeing anyone?"

Oh, my God. Seriously? AJ Harris was looking for evidence of a wedding ring on *her* finger? Her blood started to boil. "That is none of your business, but for what it's worth, no. I'm not. After you, I swore off men." She paused to catch her breath. "How many women are you currently seeing?"

He stared at her, hard. "How many? What are you talking about?"

"Oh, please. I can add and subtract. For you to have a kid who just turned two years old, you must have already been married, or seriously thinking about it, when you were screwing me."

To hell with the client always being right. This time she didn't regret saying what was on her mind, and AJ's stunned silence was her reward. "Since you couldn't be bothered to tell me about your personal life when we were sleeping together, you have no right to ask about mine now."

"Things aren't always what they seem. Not that you'd care." With that he swung around and strode out of the room.

What the hell? Had that actually been relief she'd seen in his eyes? She felt as though someone had let the air out of her tires. *Things aren't always what they seem?* What was that supposed to mean? Was he saying he wasn't married? Maybe he was in the habit of getting women pregnant and then dumping them. Maybe…

Stop it! She had a three-week job to do here and this was day one. She couldn't let AJ's cryptic comments get to her, and she sure couldn't spend the next twenty-one days making herself crazy about the past. Not his and certainly not hers.

She opened the garbage bag and started cramming strips of wallpaper into it. Work was the only way she'd learned to deal with the crappy stuff life kept throwing at her. After she cleared up the mess, she hauled the bags out to her truck and tossed them in the back. Then she climbed into the cab and dug the tuna sandwich and a bottle of water out of her lunch bag. Maybe her head would stop pounding after she put something in her stomach.

AJ PUT HERSHEY IN HIS CRATE in the laundry room while Annie settled Will into his booster seat at the kitchen table and served his lunch.

"Would you like to join us, Mr. Harris?"

"Thanks, Annie, but I'll take mine upstairs and catch up on some work. Let me know when Will's ready for a nap, though."

"I'll bring him up," she said. "By then that interior decorator girl should be here. I said I'd help her go through everything in the kitchen. You sure there isn't anything you'd especially like to keep?"

He took a long look around the cluttered room and ran a mental inventory of the cabinets' contents. "I'll need the basics for the new place. Pots, pans, dishes."

He sure didn't need his grandmother's collection of teapots—he didn't even need one—and forget about the drawers crammed with place mats, frilly aprons, knitted pot holders and God knows what else. He thought about the compact kitchen in the cabin he'd bought in northern Idaho. It had room for the basics, but that's all they would need. There were also ten acres for Will and Hershey to explore, a school bus into town when the time came and, most important, no chance of being haunted by the past. Although now that the past was staring him down, the need to escape was not so threatening and a little less urgent.

Annie handed him a plate with his favorite club sandwich and a green salad on the side. "Would you like some coffee? I just brewed a fresh pot."

"Thanks. I'll get it."

"Then you can take it into your office and get some work done while you keep an eye on that pretty young carpenter girl."

He had already moved his office upstairs, and she

knew it. He avoided making eye contact with her and concentrated on pouring coffee instead. "I don't think she needs to be supervised."

"That's not what I meant."

No, she didn't, but he knew exactly what she did mean.

Annie was undeterred by his lack of response. "I see things, you know."

He shot her a look then. He knew she *saw* things. She was the most perceptive woman he'd ever met, sometimes eerily so. She hadn't even seen him and Sam together but somehow she had figured out there was something between them. As long as she didn't figure out everything, he had nothing to worry about.

"Thanks for the sandwich. I'll take this upstairs and eat while I work."

"I see things," she called after him.

In his bedroom he set the plate and coffee cup on the desk next to his laptop. He heard the front door open and close below, followed by the sound of Sam's work boots on the floorboards of the porch. He drew back the curtain in time to see her toss a couple of garbage bags in the back of her delivery truck and close the doors.

Most women wore baggy clothes to disguise a multitude of sins. Sam wore oversize T-shirts to disguise an extremely attractive pair of feminine assets. Not too big, not too small, just about perfect. She had explained, after they'd started sleeping together and he had made a point of asking, how hard it was for a woman to be taken seriously in the construction industry. The less she looked like a woman, the better her chances. He'd thought that was a shame because as far as he was concerned, being a damn good carpenter *and* a very beautiful woman had been two counts in her favor. The blue

jeans were another matter. He was an ass man, and she
had a fine one. The snug but not-too-snug jeans she
always wore made it that much finer. Too bad those
womanly attributes hadn't extended to being a mother.

Instead of coming back inside, she opened the door
of the cab and slid in behind the wheel. Was she leaving? She unwrapped a sandwich and took a bite. No,
she was having lunch. She looked a little lost, sitting out
there alone, but better out there than inside the house.
The shock of seeing her sitting on the foyer floor, laughing with his son, had scared the hell out of him. Maybe
that's why he'd picked a fight with her. He smacked
himself on the forehead. What the hell had he been
thinking, asking her if she was seeing anyone? He had
no right to ask, and he risked everything by revisiting
their past, never mind wanting to explore their present.
He wouldn't let it happen again. He really wanted to ask
why she had broken off their relationship, even though
he knew she would never admit she was having his baby
and had no intention of keeping it.

He watched her take a sip from a water bottle. She
seemed to be staring into space, and he wondered what
she was thinking about. Damn. Her lonely vulnerability
had drawn him to her in the past, it had been something
they had in common, but he had moved beyond that
now. He wasn't alone anymore. He had Will, and he
couldn't let Sam get close to him. It's not as though
she'd figure out the truth. How could she? He'd covered
his tracks well, but his gut was telling him he needed
to be careful.

What about Annie? She was already quite taken with
"the carpenter girl." If he asked her to keep Will away
from Sam and Kristi, she would want to know why. And
although he had no intention of telling her, she would

find a way to wheedle the truth out of him. Would the truth change her opinion of Sam? It had sure as hell changed his.

After seeing her leave the lawyer's office and learning what she planned to do with the baby, he'd been sure of two things. He had to find out if the baby was his, and if it was, he wanted to be a father. He had lost everyone he'd ever loved—his brother to suicide, his mother to addiction and Sam to her own selfishness. But his child...*his son!*...he couldn't lose him. The decision, and how to make it happen, became all-consuming. Should he confront Sam? Insist on a paternity test? Melanie Morrow cautioned against it. If she refused the paternity test and contested his paternal rights, the baby would be placed in foster care until the matter was settled in court. The idea sickened him. Almost as much as he was sickened by Sam's actions. She was putting the baby up for adoption, wasn't interested in an open adoption and didn't want to have any part in the process. Melanie was screening prospective families. The final choice was hers, and for once he'd been glad he was a Harris because he'd used both the money and the position to convince Melanie to choose him.

From the moment AJ held his son and saw his older brother's face—and Sam's eyes—he had known he made the right decision. He had lost a big part of himself the day his brother had hanged himself in his bedroom at the age of sixteen. The day his son was born, he became a whole person again. He hadn't had to make a decision to his father's ultimatum. His son had made it for him.

Chapter Six

Sam unscrewed the top of her water bottle and took a swig, but her hands were shaking so badly, some of the contents sloshed down the front of her T-shirt. She dried her chin with the sleeve of her jacket and set the bottle into the cup holder.

Where the hell did he get off asking if she was going out with anyone? Her personal life, or lack of, was none of his business. And now she was every bit as furious with herself for telling him she'd sworn off men. Talk about a head-smacker. She should have told him she *was* seeing someone.

No. That wouldn't be right. He was the deceiver, but she had never lied to him. She hadn't told him about the baby, but she hadn't lied about it. So no, telling him he had no right to ask about her personal life had been the right thing to do.

She unwrapped the tuna sandwich and took an angry bite. AJ had been irked when she called him on having an affair with her while he was married to William's mother, but he hadn't denied it. How could he? It was the truth. AJ Harris was a lying, two-timing weasel who did what he pleased and didn't care who he hurt in the process.

She picked up the water bottle, hands a little steadier, and washed down the tuna and day-old bread. Who was she kidding? It had been a day old when she bought it three days ago. Yesterday on her way home from work she'd stopped to buy a quart of milk and a can of tuna. She had also bought a fresh croissant to go with her mother's tuna salad. Mrs. Stanton would be at the apartment now, and Sam hoped she'd be able to distract her mother from the jigsaw puzzle long enough to eat something. Mrs. Stanton had way more patience with Tildy Elliott than Sam did, and she usually coaxed her to eat with the promise of a homemade cookie or tart for dessert.

For most of the morning the scent of baking ginger-bread had wafted out of the kitchen and she wondered when the nanny planned to decorate the cookies with AJ's son. He was an engaging little boy, and Sam's emotional reaction to him had been the exact opposite to what she'd imagined. When it came to the son AJ had fathered with another woman, she had expected to experience cool indifference. Instead her heart had melted like butter. Will Harris had made her laugh and want to hug him. He had also made her want what she thought she had given up wanting a long time ago. A real home, a real family, someone to love and someone to love her back, unconditionally.

Sam-I-am. She smiled at that. The little boy had connected her to his favorite story, a book she remembered from her own childhood, although she had no recollection of anyone having read it to her. For sure no one had ever made her green eggs and ham.

She had never spent time around small children, so she hadn't known what to expect of a little boy who had "just turned two." Did her son have a puppy? A favorite story? A favorite food? Of course he did. He had two devoted parents, a home filled with love. She had left the job of finding him the perfect family to her lawyer because she hadn't been able to deal with making those decisions herself. Instead she simply believed he had all those things and more, because if he didn't...

Don't go there, she warned herself. Her son—she always thought of him as James, AJ's middle name, even though she hadn't formally named him when he was born—had everything she never had, and more. Without AJ in her life, there was no way she could care for a baby and her mother and go to work every day, and as her due date drew closer, she had made her decision. By then the deeply rooted anger she'd harbored toward AJ for sending his father to deal with her had been downgraded to loathing. She had never felt guilty for not telling him about the baby, knowing he wouldn't want the burden of her child any more than he'd wanted her. Now, especially seeing how he was with his son, she wasn't so sure. Maybe if she had told him, he would have changed his mind and—

Idiot! He'd already had a wife.

She picked up the other half of her sandwich and decided she couldn't choke down another bite if she tried, so she wrapped it up and zipped it into her lunch bag. If she got hungry later on, she could take a break and eat it then. With any luck AJ would be away from the house again this afternoon and she could relax instead of jumping every time she saw her shadow.

God, she wanted to hate him. She certainly had every right to. Seeing him again brought back a lot of memories, though. In particular the memory that she had loved him once. They'd had a connection, a powerful one, and although he would undoubtedly deny it now, she knew he'd felt it, too. He'd been hurt by something, badly hurt, as she had been, and the scars ran deep. Neither had wanted to talk about the past, and neither had expected it of the other.

AJ was a man of few words, but he'd spoken the intimate language of love with his hands, his mouth, his body, as passionate in the bedroom as he was reserved in the boardroom. The memory of making love with him heated Sam's insides. When he stripped away her clothes, he had taken a lifetime of hurt and disappointment with them. In AJ's bed, she wasn't the crazy lady's daughter or the girl who'd been abandoned by her father. She was "sexy Sam." He'd whispered it once, just before making her come, and the words still echoed in her head.

She was in the middle of giving herself a silent pep talk, along with a reminder to get back to work, when Kristi's van pulled up behind her truck. Reinforcements had arrived. Sam climbed out of her truck and waved.

Kristi waved back and stepped out of her van. She was wearing her typical work clothes—a fuchsia-colored hoodie, black yoga pants that ended midcalf and pink sneakers. Her blond hair was pulled into a ponytail. "Hi! How's it going?"

Sam zipped her jacket to block the damp chill. "Good. I was just eating my lunch."

"In your truck?"

Sam shrugged. "I didn't want to get in the way." She hiked a thumb in the direction of the house. "Interfere with...you know...the family and stuff."

"We'll work something out," Kristi said. "When I'm putting in full days here, I'm not sitting outside to have lunch. It's freezing." She slid open the side door of her van. "Can you give me a hand with these things?"

"Sure." Sam helped her unload plastic storage bins, a roll of packing paper and a carryall crammed with labels, markers and tape—the tools of Kristi's trade.

Sam hauled the bins onto the veranda while Kristi slung her carryall over her shoulder and followed.

"How's it going with AJ?" Kristi asked. "Have you seen him today?"

"He was out this morning, but I ran into him before lunch. I didn't really have a chance to talk to him."

Kristi paused at the top of the front steps. "So you ran into him, but you didn't talk."

"That's right. Why?"

"I'm worried about you." Kristi set her bag on the porch and flung an arm around Sam's shoulders. "Give me a hand getting this stuff into the kitchen and I promise…no more questions."

Right. I'll believe that when I see it, Sam thought.

MIDAFTERNOON, KRISTI breezed through the foyer with a plastic bin in her arms.

"One down, a dozen more to go." She juggled the bin with one arm and opened the door. "I'm just running this out to my van. Be back in a few minutes," she said, leaving the front door ajar.

Sam was climbing down the stepladder as Will raced through the room, making a beeline for the open door.

"Whoa, little man. Where do you think you're going?" Sam scooped the little boy into her arms.

"Out!" His soft brown curls and the scent of baby powder tickled her nose.

"Not by yourself, you're not. Where's your nanny?"

"Sleeping."

Sam doubted that. She also found it hard to believe the child had slipped under Annie Dobson's radar. After one day in this house, Sam was certain the woman had eyes in the back of her head.

"Where's your dad?"

"Sleeping."

Little trickster. "Then we'd better go wake them up."

His sturdy little body fit nicely against her hip as she carried him down the hallway to the kitchen. "Why?"

"So you can tell them what you're doing. Where's your puppy?" she asked, purposefully changing the subject.

"Sleeping."

There might actually be some truth to that. "Why aren't you sleeping?"

"I going out."

"You're too little to go out by yourself."

"I'm a *big* boy." He flung his arms wide to demonstrate.

"You sure are, but we still need to find your nanny."

"Why?"

"Because maybe she'll give you—" She stopped herself before she said "cookie." "Because she's probably looking for you." She hoped he didn't ask why because she was running out of answers.

He didn't, thank goodness. Instead he laughed and covered his eyes. "Can't find me!" Then he spread two fingers to make a narrow slit and peeked at her.

The cuteness was almost unbearable. She gave his ribs a little tickle. "I can see you."

The fingers snapped shut again and he giggled. "Not now!"

She carried him into the kitchen and set him on the counter, keeping her hands on either side of him so he couldn't fall. "Hmm, I wonder what happened to William," she said. "I can't find him anywhere."

Was he still young enough to believe that covering his eyes made him invisible or did he simply enjoy the game? And then she realized it didn't matter because she was enjoying it, too.

"What are you doing?"

Sam practically jumped out of her skin at the sound of AJ's voice. She was suddenly gripped by guilt, although she had no idea why. She wasn't doing anything wrong, she was looking out for his little boy when no one else was. "I...um...the front door was open and he was trying to follow Kristi outside. I'm sorry. We'll be more careful." She lifted the child off the counter and set him on the floor. "Here's your dad," she said to him.

The softening of AJ's stony expression was almost imperceptible. "Come here, Will."

The child's curls bounced as he shook his head and took Sam's hand. "We playing." His brown-eyed gaze melted her heart. "Right?"

She wrapped her fingers around the small, warm hand and nodded because her throat had gone tight and she couldn't speak.

"Come here," AJ repeated. "Where's your nanny?"

"Sleeping." Will's hand tightened on Sam's.

His father slowly advanced on them. "Sorry about this. I thought he was upstairs with Annie. Come on, Will. Let's go look for her."

The child laughed and darted behind Sam's legs. "Can't see me!"

AJ was getting closer. "We have to let Sam get back to work."

Before he could get any nearer, Sam swung around and scooped the child into her arms. "Gotcha, you little rascal." She turned back to AJ, relieved he'd stopped a few feet away, dismayed by his solemn expression.

Was he upset with his son for misbehaving, or with her for…what? Being here?

The child, oblivious to his father's disapproval, squealed with laughter, and she had to tighten her hold on the wriggling body so she didn't drop him.

AJ came another step closer and reached for his son, but Will wrapped his arms around Sam's neck.

Not sure what else to do, she moved toward AJ so he could take the child.

The circle of Will's arms tightened around her.

The stroke of AJ's hands against the sides of her neck, as he gently grasped the boy's arms and moved them away, sent delicious shivers down her spine.

"No! I playing with Sam-I-am!"

AJ, clearly exasperated, slid one hand around Will's chest at the exact same moment the child flung himself at Sam once again. The back of AJ's hand against her breast had an electrifying effect—on both of them, judging by his expression—but instead of being jolted apart, they were locked in the moment. Even Will stopped squirming.

"There you are." Annie Dobson's voice released the tension and they quickly pulled apart. This time, Will was in AJ's embrace.

Annie's gaze darted between AJ and Sam, and then her mouth spread into a smile. "Well, isn't this nice." She bustled into the room and took the boy from AJ. "It's a relief he didn't get into any trouble. He fell asleep on my bed while we were reading and then I took out my knitting, but I must've nodded off, too. When I woke up, the little scallywag was gone."

So, Will had been telling the truth about the nanny being asleep. Sam glanced at AJ to see what his reaction would be, but he seemed preoccupied.

Kristi sauntered back into the kitchen, carrying two empty plastic bins. "Oh, good, you're both here," she said to Annie and AJ. "I need to know what you'd like me to do with all the stuff I left on the kitchen table before I…" Her voice trailed off as she became aware of the tension in the room. She deposited the bins on the table next to a pile of kitchen gadgets and raised an eyebrow at Sam.

That's when Sam realized AJ was still standing next to her. "I have to get back to work," she said, inching away from him. "Carry on." When she reached the doorway, she turned and fled to the foyer.

She picked up the putty knife and dropped it because her hands were shaking, badly. She picked it up again and stood there a moment, trying to calm her breathing. The skin on her neck tingled where AJ had touched her, and every ounce of her sizzled when she recalled the firm pressure of his hand on her breast. Oh, God. This was not good. He had lied to her and cheated on his wife. His father had threatened to put her out of work. She could *not* be lusting after AJ Harris.

Three weeks. The work on the house would be finished in three weeks and she could get back to her normal routine of working and caring for her mother. This house would be sold, he and his little boy would move to Idaho and she would never have to worry about running into him again.

The next three weeks would be hell, though. There would be constant reminders of how she had once been completely and madly in love with him, and there would be constant reminders of the child she'd given up. Until today she had never held a child, not even her own baby, and now her heart ached like it never had before. She dropped the knife into the bucket of putty, sat down at the bottom of the stairs and buried her face in her hands.

"Sweetie, what is it? Are you okay?" Kristi came in, sat next to her and put an arm around her shoulders.

Sam lowered her hands and dabbed at the corners of her eyes with her shirtsleeve. "I'm fine. I just didn't expect this to be so—"

"Hard?"

Sam sniffed.

Kristi pulled a packet of tissues out of her pocket and handed one to her.

"Thanks. You're such a mom."

"And men can be such jerks," Kristi said.

Sam dabbed the moisture from her eyes and blew her nose. "For the record, I'm not crying."

"Of course you're not." Kristi grinned at her. "A little weepy, maybe, but definitely not crying. I would be, too, if I found out I had to work for my ex. Not that anything of the sort could ever happen to me. He's either holed up in some scuzzy apartment or he's been evicted and had to resort to couch surfing. Compared to me, you have very good taste in men, which would work in your favor if *all* men weren't jerks."

Sam tossed the tissue into a trash bag and shook her head at Kristi. "It's not AJ, it's me. I thought I was over him, I *am* over him, but…oh, hell. I don't know. This was unexpected and I'm overreacting."

"Don't be so hard on yourself. You were completely blindsided. Like Claire said yesterday, if this is too difficult for you, we can—"

"I'll be fine." She'd have to be, because no way would she give him the satisfaction of running her off a second time. "I just wish…" She wished he didn't have a child, but she couldn't say it out loud. Kristi would want to know why, and that was one secret she would never share.

"You wish…?"

"I wish it was Christmas." She had to say something.

"Really? You don't even like Christmas."

True, she didn't. What was there to like? She'd haul the shabby three-foot-tall prelit artificial tree out of their storage locker in the basement, buy a canned ham and fill two Christmas stockings with gifts—one for her mother and one for herself. For the past two years, since opening the business, she, Kristi and Claire got together for dinner the week before Christmas to relax, celebrate their partnership and exchange gifts. For Sam it had become the highlight of the holiday. Before that, she couldn't remember when she'd last received a real present.

"I'm not the biggest fan of decking the halls and ho ho ho," she admitted. "But we'll be finished this job before Christmas, and that's what I'm looking forward to." And never having to see AJ and his son again. She pushed up her sleeve and checked her watch. "I appreciate you talking me down."

"You'd do the same for me. That's what friends are for."

Now, if only friends could speed up time. "I need to get back to work," she said. "There's so much to do before I can call it a day, and I really want to get out of here."

"Look at the bright side," Kristi said. "Day one is almost over."

One down, twenty to go. Sam figured she'd be more likely to see the bright side when those numbers were reversed.

Chapter Seven

The next morning Sam unloaded her painting supplies onto the front porch and used her front-door key to let herself in. The house was quiet but filled with the scent of something warm and chocolaty. She sniffed again. And a hint of banana, too? She went back out for the tarps, careful to close the door in case AJ's son was on the loose.

An aproned Annie Dobson stood in the foyer when she went back inside.

"Good morning, dear. How are you this morning? You just missed Mr. Harris and young William. They've taken the dog out for their morning walk. Would you like a cup of tea and a muffin before you get started? They're fresh out of the oven and still warm." She paused for a breath, smiling broadly.

If the muffin had anything to do with the scent of chocolate-and-banana heaven, how could she say no? Especially knowing a trip to the kitchen would not involve a run-in with AJ. "I have a lot of work to do today, but tea and a muffin sound great."

"Come on down to the kitchen and help yourself. If you like, you can bring them back here to have while you work."

To stay on schedule she needed to finish the foyer today, but she also wanted to ask Annie how to bake gingerbread cookies. Maybe even score the recipe. She piled the tarps on the floor and closed the door. "Lead the way."

Annie Dobson was so typically nannyish, she could be on a film set. This morning her blue-green-and-black pleated tartan skirt was matched with a white blouse under a royal-blue cardigan. Her legs and feet were clad in thick tan-colored stockings and a pair of sensible dark brown oxfords. The woman's ankles were almost as wide as her calves, like two sturdy fence posts, but they sure didn't impede her ability to get around. Sam picked up her pace as she followed Annie to the kitchen.

"Have a seat. I'll get you a cup."

A red-white-and-black teapot shaped like a rooster sat in the middle of the table. One of many from AJ's grandmother's collection, Sam assumed. Kristi had admired them and decided they should stay in the kitchen, on display in one of the glass-doored upper cabinets. Sam's mother, always fond of tea parties, would love them. And a new teapot would make the perfect Christmas present, Sam decided.

Annie bustled about, and within moments Sam was served a steaming cup of Earl Grey tea in an old-fashioned rose-patterned china cup and saucer, and a warm banana chocolate-chunk muffin on a matching plate.

"Mmm, this is delicious," she said after swallowing her first mouthful and taking a sip of the fragrant tea.

"Glad you like it, dear. I have to say, this kitchen is already much easier to work in now that Kristi has started clearing out Mrs. Harris's things. She was a delightful old girl, as you very well know, but she never wanted to get rid of anything. 'You never know when it'll come in handy' is what she always used to say, and Mr. Harris liked to humor her."

As you very well know? Where had that come from? "Um, I never met AJ's…I mean Mr. Harris's grand-mother."

"Really? Oh, well, I just assumed. The two of you seem to have a thing for each other."

Sam, about to take another bite of her muffin, set it back on the plate instead. Was it *that* obvious?

Annie flashed a smile. "I pick up on things like this."

So had Claire and Kristi. She had to be careful be-cause there were things she didn't want anyone to pick up on. Not Claire and Kristi, not Annie Dobson and certainly not AJ.

"AJ and I met when I did some work for his father. It was a long time ago."

Annie sharpened her gaze by narrowing her eyes.

Sam squirmed a little.

"Old man Harris never shows his face around here and neither does AJ's mother. They're the poorer for it, if you ask me." She started filling the sink with hot water and added a squirt of detergent. "Sorry. It's not my place to gossip about Mr. Harris's family."

Annie probably didn't know the half of it. Curious, though, that AJ's parents were no longer part of his life. From where she'd stood, the Harris family had been tight-knit to the point of being impenetrable, especially by someone like her. What could have happened to change that? Then again, it had been AJ's father who'd made a point of saying "there are places for people like your mother."

"I'm sorry to hear that," Sam said, although the child

was probably better off without such an overbearing grandfather.

Annie picked up the teapot and carried it back to the counter. "They're the ones who're missing out on watching young William grow up. He's the apple of his daddy's eye, and you'd think his grandparents—" She paused and shook her head. "There I go again. You're not interested in hearing me natter on about this." She rinsed the teapot and turned off the tap.

On one hand Sam wanted to know more, but on the other she didn't want to raise any more suspicions than Annie already had.

"This muffin is delicious," Sam said instead. "I was wondering, if you don't mind, if I could have your recipe for making gingerbread men."

Annie faced her again, this time with a warm smile, her indiscretion already forgotten. "Of course, dear. You've never made them before?"

"I've never baked cookies, ever."

"Your mother never taught you how to bake?"

"Oh, um, my mom's really not well, healthwise I mean. I'd like to get her to help me, though. She might enjoy it." As long as she was having a good day.

If the revelation surprised Annie, she didn't let on. "I'm sorry to hear that, dear. Of course you can have it. I'll write it out on a recipe card and give it to you before you go home today."

"Thanks."

"Do you have everything you need? Rolling pin? Cookie sheets?"

Hmm. There weren't many kitchens as poorly equipped as hers. "I'll have to check when I get home."

"That sounds like a 'no' to me."

Instead of being off-putting, Annie's matter-of-factness made Sam laugh. "You're right. It's a definite no." She picked up her cup and drank the last of her tea.

"Not to worry, dear. Kristi and I are clearing out the pantry today…all the baking utensils are kept in there…and I'm sure we'll find extras. Which reminds me, I need to keep an eye out for cake pans and set those aside. I'll need to make young William's birthday cake in a couple of weeks."

Sam's cup clattered onto the saucer, drawing a sharp look from Annie.

"Sorry. Clumsy me." But seriously, William, AJ's son, had a birthday in *a couple of weeks?* Kristi had asked how old the boy was, and Sam was sure AJ had said he had just turned two. Is that what he'd said? Or had he said the boy was *just two,* meaning he hadn't yet turned three? For AJ to have a son the same age as hers, he had definitely been cheating on his wife with Sam. Is that why he'd misled them about his son's age?

From across the kitchen, Annie was watching her like a hawk. "Something wrong, dear?"

Either nothing was wrong or everything was wrong, and there was only one way to find out. "Everything's fine. That'll be fun. The birthday, I mean. Um…" She had to know. "When is it?"

"December fifteenth." Annie seemed to be waiting for her reaction.

She struggled to stay calm, even though the date knocked the breath out of her. Of all the bizarre coincidences, William and her son—*both* of AJ's sons—were born on the same day. There was no longer any doubt that he'd been sleeping with her and Will's mother at the same time. Still, for his wife to have a baby on the same day she did…it was crazy.

What if…?

*You're the one who's crazy. There's no way William
is* your *son.*

Unless…had AJ found out she was pregnant? She
didn't see how. *They found out about your mother,* she
reminded herself.

"They grow so quickly. It's hard to believe he's almost three." Annie had turned back to the sink.

Did Annie know more than she let on? Whether she
did or not, this wasn't the time to ply her with questions. First, Sam needed time to think, to come up with
a plan. She carefully pushed the cup and saucer and the
plate containing half a muffin toward the center of the
table and stood up, taking the opportunity to make her
getaway. "Thank you for the tea and the muffin. It was
delicious, but I really have to get to work now."

She walked to the foyer and stared at the tarps and
paint cans for what felt like forever. Could she do this?
Could she spend the next three weeks here, working for
AJ, not knowing if William was his child or if he was…
theirs? The possibility was preposterous, but now that
she suspected it, she had to know for sure. The problem
was how to get the answers she was looking for. If she
asked AJ, would he be honest? No way, not if he had
something to hide.

Snippets of recent events flashed through her mind.
AJ had been reluctant to take them into the kitchen that
first day, when Will was out in the yard. He'd made a
vague reference to the child's age. He was awkward
and edgy when she and Will were in the same room
together. Was it because he felt guilty for cheating on
his wife? Or was it something even more underhanded?

DINNER IN THE HARRIS kitchen that evening felt different
and oddly unsettling. AJ wanted to attribute his mood

to the changes Sam and Kristi had made in a mere two days—they had swept in like a pair of commandos and their progress was impressive. The countertops were all but bare, the curtains removed for cleaning and the vintage knickknacks taken to a consignment shop. Who knew people would pay good money for that stuff? The only reminders that this had been his grandmother's kitchen were the teapots now on display and the row of potted African violets on the windowsill. Annie loved the plants and wanted to keep them, so before the Ready Set Sold women staged the house for sale, they planned to convert his office back into a sunroom and display the plants in there until Annie was ready to take them with her.

These changes were all for the better, but tonight he didn't feel better. Instead, anxiety gnawed at his gut like a hungry sewer rat. He'd already had two, not one but *two,* run-ins with Sam. The first had rattled him emotionally. The second had left him physically shaken and, damn it, fully aroused.

Will's reaction to her troubled him even more. AJ had seen the way his son had wrapped his arms around Sam's neck and clung to her, he'd watched the gentle way she had held Will—and both scared the hell out of him. Was it possible for a mother and child to have a bond, even though they didn't know one another? No. That's the kind of thing Annie would believe. As far as he was concerned it was a load of crap. His own mother was living proof that some women never bonded with their children. But Sam and Will…God, what was that about?

Sam had no idea who Will was. Will wasn't old enough to understand he even had a mother. In spite of Annie's attempts to "broaden the child's horizons," AJ had deliberately kept him from activities that involved other children and their parents. That would change only when they were settled in their new home in Idaho, when all this was behind them and AJ had figured out how to answer the inevitable questions about his son's mother.

AJ watched Annie settle Will in his booster seat and slid his chair closer to the table. "Here you go, young man. Eat your dinner."

Across the kitchen, the dog eagerly devoured his daily allotment of kibble. "Hawshey eats his dinner."

"That's right. Now you be a good boy like Hershey and eat up."

In spite of the renovation chaos, Annie had managed to whip up a salad, meatloaf, mashed potatoes and peas, and he knew there'd be something delicious for dessert. There always was. He was definitely going to miss her cooking.

Annie sat across the table from him, spectacles perched on the end of her nose, and stared at him intently. "So, are you happy with that young woman you hired?"

Here we go. He'd have to be a complete moron to miss the subtext. She wasn't referring to the "team of professionals" from Ready Set Sold, she was talking about Sam. It was unfortunate she'd come into the room at the exact moment that he and Sam were having a moment.

"They're doing a good job," he said, choosing his words carefully. "The kitchen looks great, don't you think?"

She made a point of glancing around the room, giving him a respite from her steely gray gaze. "It does. I never realized how many unnecessary things were in here till they were gone. Same goes for the foyer, don't you think? Sam works fast."

More subtext.

"Sam-I-am," Will said, picking up a pea with his fingers and popping it in his mouth. "I like Sam-I-am."

Will didn't know if his son referred to the Dr. Seuss character or the hammer-wielding heartbreaker, and he didn't ask. He might not like the answer.

Annie purposefully placed Will's fork in his hand, picked up her own without looking at him and sampled the mashed potatoes.

AJ had no appetite at all but he couldn't think of a reason to excuse himself, so he lowered his head and started eating. The sooner he cleared his plate, the sooner he could slip upstairs on the pretext of having work to do. Which was true, he did. Having Sam here had proved to be a major distraction, and if he hoped to meet his Friday deadline, he'd have to work tonight and find a way to avoid distractions tomorrow. And the next day, and the next…

The tags on Hershey's collar jangled against the stainless-steel water bowl.

Will laughed at that, as he always did, and picked up his glass of milk with one hand. "I drinking like Hawshey."

Annie steadied his arm. "You need to use two hands."

Will shook his head and the milk sloshed from side to side in the glass. That, AJ knew, was why Annie filled it only half-full. "One hand," Will said. "I a big boy."

He said that a lot these days, and it was true. The toddler who had once relied on his father for everything was quickly transforming into a child with a determined spirit and a mind of his own. William was so much like his uncle and namesake, both in looks and personality, that at times it took AJ's breath away. If only there were some way to slow the clock.

Growing up, AJ had been the quiet, reserved one, the kid with few friends who'd kept to himself. His brother, William, had been confident and outgoing, always part of a large social circle. When Will was old enough to go to school, AJ had a feeling he'd be a lot like his uncle.

When William had turned fifteen, though, there had been an abrupt change in his personality. It was as if someone had flipped a switch and the older sibling he'd looked up to and adored and desperately tried to emulate suddenly withdrew from everyone and everything around him. Silent and moody, he spent long hours behind the closed door of his bedroom, shutting out everyone, even AJ.

A year later he had taken his own life, leaving AJ angry with his parents for ignoring his brother's depression and covering up his suicide, and guilt-ridden for not finding someone who would listen to his concerns about the drastic change in his brother. He'd buried the guilt and anger long ago, deep enough inside that he didn't need to feel them, but they had never disappeared.

Will was a lot like his mother, too, and today that unexpected discovery had landed on AJ like a load of lumber. Sam and Will had the same soft brown eyes, the same sense of purpose. AJ still vividly remembered the day he'd gone to see her, against the lawyer's advice, to confront her about the pregnancy and the paternity of her soon-to-be-born baby, and had met her mother instead. It had been clear, almost immediately, that the woman suffered from some type of mental illness. Sam had never talked about her, had never even mentioned her family, and he'd never told her about his, either.

Now watching his son happily eating and chattering with his nanny about the dog and what they were going to do tomorrow, he allowed himself to surrender to one of those rare moments when he pondered the possibility that the mental illnesses that had cast a cloud over his family, and Sam's, might inflict themselves on his son. Were these things hereditary? He loved his son more than he'd ever thought it possible to love another human being, but that would never cloud his judgment. If Will ever showed signs of sinking into a depression the way AJ's brother had, they would get help.

Will's fork clattered to the table. "All done. Go play with Hawshey."

The dog was sprawled on the mat by the back door. Now that his belly was full, he wouldn't be feeling very playful, but he would tolerate Will's attempts to coax him into some escapade.

AJ stood and slid his son's chair away from the table. "What do you say to Annie?"

"Good dinner!"

"Thank you, sweet boy. Go play with your dog while I tidy up the kitchen. Then it's bath and bedtime."

Will scampered across the kitchen and crouched next to Hershey. "Time to wake up."

AJ stacked his plate on Will's and carried them to the sink. "It was a very good dinner. It's also been a long day, and you've more than earned a night off. I'll clean up and get Will ready for bed." He was still feeling distracted and knew if he tried to work, he would end up only staring at the computer screen and thinking about Sam.

"You still have work to do."

"I do, but this won't take long."

Annie had already rinsed her plate and loaded it into

the dishwasher. "All I plan to do tonight is watch TV and work on the sweater I'm knitting William for his birthday."

He set the plates on the counter before he dropped them. Will's birthday was ten days before Christmas. He had circumvented the subject of his son's age when one of Sam's partners had asked. According to the schedule they'd given him, they would be finished with the house and out of here before Will's birthday. Damn it, what if they weren't? If Sam found out Will's birthday, his cover would be blown. Sam assumed he'd been cheating on Will's mother by having an affair with her, and he needed for her to keep believing that. For that to happen, she could not find out Will's birth date. Did he dare try to enlist Annie's help with that? When it came to Will's well-being, he trusted her implicitly, but could he ask her to lie?

He watched her bustle around the kitchen in her tartan skirt and sensible brown lace-up oxfords. Exactly how did one ask the most down-to-earth, honest and decent person on the planet to lie?

One didn't. He tried to fill his lungs with air and they fought back. He needed a better plan than that.

"We should probably keep the birthday plans on the down-low." He kept his voice quiet on the pretext of not letting Will hear him. "You know how wound up he gets about these things. It might be better to surprise him."

Annie's back seemed to stiffen as she picked up the plates he'd set on the counter. "There's nothing wrong with little boys getting excited about having a birthday."

She had a lot more experience with kids than he did, but that wasn't the point. "You're right," he said. "It doesn't have to be a surprise, but maybe he doesn't need to hear about it until a day or two beforehand."

"Of course, Mr. Harris. If that's what you'd like, then that's what we'll do." Her tone, suddenly distant and formal, made him a little uneasy. "And I know you have things that need taking care of. I can manage here, and I'll bring young William in to say good-night when he's ready for bed."

Things that need taking care of. It sounded cryptic, and he couldn't tell if she meant to say he had *work* that needed taking care of or if she suspected he was up to something. But that was crazy. How could she?

AFTER SAM CHECKED IN with Mrs. Stanton, who said Tildy was having a "good day," she quietly let herself into the apartment. Her mother had apparently finished the puzzle, ate a little of the tuna salad Sam had left for her, plus a generous slice of Mrs. Stanton's homemade apple pie, and had talked about having tea. Sam didn't ask if the queen was still the guest of honor, and Mrs. Stanton didn't say. As usual at this time of day, the television was blaring.

"Mom? I'm home."

"I'm in here, dear."

Sam unlaced her boots, tugged them off and wriggled her toes. She stowed the boots in the closet, then carried her clipboard into the kitchen and set it on the counter along with her lunch bag. She needed to go over her supply lists for tomorrow, but that would have to wait until after supper. Right now she desperately wanted a shower. First she went into the living room.

Tildy was wearing the green-and-gold silk, an indication that Her Majesty had *appeared* as anticipated. Her mother had also applied more makeup than she'd been wearing that morning, and the two bright spots of color on her cheeks, toned down by a generous dusting of powder, matched her glossy red lips.

Sam sat next to her and gave her a hug. "You look beautiful." And she meant it. To the rest of the world her mother might seem a little crazy—okay, a *lot* crazy—but this had always been Sam's normal, and after the emotional roller coaster she'd endured today, her mother's brand of reality was like a breath of fresh air.

"How was your day, Mom? Did Mrs. Stanton come over?"

"We had lunch together," her mother said without taking her eyes off the TV. "She brought pie. Did you remember to buy milk?"

"Yes," she lied. "I put it in the fridge."

"Oh, good. What's for dinner?"

She wished she could say they were having meatloaf. That's what Annie Dobson had put in the oven before Sam and Kristi had called it a day, and it had smelled heavenly. "Spaghetti with tomato sauce, but first I'm going to take a shower."

"Oh, good. I've always liked Italian food."

Plain old pasta with a jar of store-bought sauce hardly qualified as "Italian," but if it satisfied some illusion of sophistication for her mother, then they were both happy. With any luck there was still enough lettuce to make them each a small salad, plus a leaf or two to go in Sam's sandwich tomorrow. She left her mother watching a rerun of *Friends,* "The One with Phoebe's Dad," and went down the short hallway to her room.

She had the smaller of the two bedrooms, but it was plenty big for her, with a single bed and a small dresser that doubled as a bedside table. She closed the door and leaned against it, head throbbing and eyelids pressed tight against the tears. After a minute or two she opened them and surveyed the room with a critical eye. A single mother could not raise a child in an environment like this. Besides, Will Harris was not her son. He couldn't be. Her son lived in a nice house with his family and a dog, and maybe even a nanny. Everything AJ's son had. Except her son had a mother. He just had to.

She wiped her eyes on the sleeve of her shirt before she methodically unhooked her cell phone from her waistband, emptied her pockets and put everything on top of the dresser. Then she stripped off her work clothes, stuffed them into the laundry hamper in her closet and pulled on an old terry cloth bathrobe to offset the cool air in her room.

The laundry was starting to pile up. She checked for quarters in the old coffee cup she kept on the dresser. Not enough to do a load tonight, but she'd remember to get change tomorrow and haul a load down to the laundry room in the basement after work. She hated going down there. It was dimly lit and smelled like soap and dirty socks. She was too tired to do laundry tonight anyway. Not bone tired as she sometimes was after a day of hard work—stripping wallpaper and patching plaster had made for a relatively easy day—but the en-counters with AJ had left her physically drained and mentally exhausted. A lot like a limp rag that had been run through the wringer. But the interaction with Will Harris had taken the greatest toll.

He was a beautiful boy, full of life and laughter, and after AJ had pried his arms off her neck and taken him upstairs, Sam felt as though her insides had been squeezed out and there was nothing left of her but a hollow shell. She'd had that same emptiness when she'd come home from the hospital, alone, and it had lasted for weeks.

Will was a miniature carbon copy of his father—the same dark hair, tall for his age, at least according to Kristi—and he'd certainly get his height from AJ. He didn't have his father's eyes, though. AJ had blue eyes that bordered on navy when his pupils dilated. Will's eyes were a soft, gentle brown, probably like his mother's.

Like her own, maybe? Sam stared at her reflection in the mirror. Everyone had always said Sam had her father's eyes. She opened her top drawer, uncovered a small metal box and took out the only photograph she had of her father. But instead of seeing her father's eyes, she was gazing into Will Harris's.

Snap out of it, you're being an idiot. She tucked the photo away, snapped the lid of the box shut and shoved the drawer into place. She'd feel better after she had a shower and something to eat.

The phone on her dresser was buzzing when she returned from the bathroom, toweling her damp hair. It was Claire.

"Sorry I didn't make it over to the Harris house today. After the open house this morning I spent the afternoon showing condos to some new clients. First-timers. At the end of the day they decided to go back and look at the first one they saw, and I think they're going to make an offer on it."

"That's great." Sam tossed the towel on her bed and opened a dresser drawer.

"How'd it go today?"

"Good. The foyer is stripped and the plaster's patched and ready to be sanded and painted tomorrow. Kristi's already made a lot of progress in the kitchen and—"

"She told me. I talked to her already."

"Right." Sam had a pretty good idea they'd talked about more than the house.

"And…how'd it go with AJ?" Claire asked, confirming her suspicion.

Sam pulled an old sweatshirt and a pair of faded flannel pajama pants out of the drawer and kneed it shut. "I suppose Kristi told you I had a bit of a meltdown."

"She was worried about you."

"I'm fine. It's just—" She couldn't say she was more upset about what Annie had said than what AJ had done, so she tried to brush it all aside. "The whole situation's a little awkward, but I can handle it."

"Kristi said he made you cry."

Sam dug in her top drawer for clean underwear. "No, he didn't." She had managed that all by herself. "We had a bit of a run-in, that's all." Two run-ins that had left her angry, not to mention hot and bothered, and hating herself for it.

"You know you don't have to do this," Claire said. "There's no way I could work for my soon-to-be ex-husband."

At first she'd been determined to do this job to show AJ she was over him and he no longer meant anything to her. Now, until she found out the truth about Will, her reasons for being there were stronger than ever.

"Kristi pretty much said the same thing, but this is different. AJ and I weren't married." Ha, not even close. "We only had a brief…whatever." She'd been about to say "relationship," but she had to stop thinking of it that way. People who were in a relationship were honest with one another. She and AJ had been caught up in a lie. "It's not like we were ever really serious."

"But, sweetie, you were in love with him. Anyone can see that."

It bugged her that her past feelings for him were so obvious. Had he picked up on it? Most men weren't that perceptive, but AJ wasn't most men. "I'm not anymore. I'll be fine. And tomorrow will be a short day because after I'm done sanding and priming the walls in the foyer, I'm going out to the warehouse to check out the old light fixtures I've salvaged. If there's nothing I can use, I'll have to go shopping."

"Good plan. Will you still be there at noon? I'd like to drop by and take a look, and I told Kristi I'd take some of the stuff she'd packed up to the consignment store."

"I sure will. I'll see you then."

"I'll bring lunch," Claire said.

"That's okay. I'll be brown-bagging."

Claire laughed. "I've seen what's in your brown bags. I was thinking more along the lines of sushi. My treat."

"You don't have to—"

"Of course I don't *have* to. I *want* to."

Sam didn't want to accept, but arguing with Claire was futile. Besides, she loved fresh sushi. "Lunch will be great."

And it would be. All day her senses had been tickled by the scents wafting from AJ's kitchen. The muffins had been followed by a simmering pot of chicken soup at lunchtime and then, later in the afternoon, the meatloaf. Who knew meatloaf smelled so good? And it was anyone's guess how Annie managed to whip up all those things in a construction zone.

Sam's stomach growled. She slipped off her bathrobe and pulled on clean underwear and the clothes she'd laid out on the bed. Tonight she'd settle for plain old spaghetti and tomato sauce, but this weekend she would make time to bake gingerbread men. In the afternoon, when she'd gone into the kitchen to refill her water bottle, Will and his nanny had been having a grand time decorating theirs with icing and candy sprinkles. Annie had even made little holes at the top of each head before she baked them so they could string the cookies with ribbon and hang them on their Christmas tree.

Sam and Tildy had never baked cookies, and since childhood she had learned to accept her mother for who she was. But what was stopping her from learning to make them, and getting her mother involved, too? It might even become a family tradition. And why not? There was a first time for everything. She could even box up some of the cookies and give them to Kristi and Claire for Christmas.

Annie had told her to drop by the kitchen at the end of the day to get the gingerbread recipe, but Sam had been so tired and completely distracted, she'd forgotten all about it. Tomorrow she'd make a point of talking to Annie, alone. She would ask about the cookie recipe, and she'd find a way to slip in a few other questions, too.

Chapter Eight

Sam's truck and Kristi's minivan were parked in front of the house when AJ and Will returned from their morning walk to the park with Hershey. He had intentionally timed their outing so they wouldn't be there when the women arrived, and now he wished they'd stayed out longer. The pup was showing signs of tiring, though, and Will had already mentioned the morning snack that Annie always had ready and waiting for him.

His son's rubber boots slapped against the damp sidewalk, his mittened hand held securely in AJ's. Annie had insisted that Will wear his winter jacket and rain pants over his jeans, and it was a good thing because he'd spent a lot of time rolling on the grass with Hershey.

AJ knew Sam was still working at the front of the house, so decided it best to sneak through the side gate and use the back door. Okay, not *sneak,* exactly. This was his house and he could use any door he liked, but it would be better to keep Will and the dog away from her. And it would have been a solid plan if she hadn't chosen that moment to open the front door and step out onto the porch. Her short dark hair was covered by a white painter's cap, worn backward, and she had on her usual jeans and work shirt.

"Sam-I-am!" Will tugged his hand free, leaving AJ holding nothing but his mitten, and dashed for the front steps.

She was reaching for a five-gallon pail of paint when she saw them, and she froze in her tracks.

"I walking my d—" The toe of Will's boot snagged the top step.

Sam dropped the handle of the paint pail and reached for him, but Will fell, face-first, onto the floorboards of the porch before she caught him. She was lifting him to his feet when the howling started. She crouched next to him. "Are you okay?"

AJ raced up the stairs with Hershey in tow and knelt beside them. "Let's have a look."

"Sorry," Sam said. "I tried to grab him."

AJ pulled off his son's hat, checked his face and the one bare hand for scrapes or bruises and found none. "He'll be okay. Won't you, Will?"

Will's howl turned to a loud whimper. "No! I fall down."

Hershey poked the front of Will's jacket with his snout as AJ stroked the brown curls off his son's forehead. "You took a little tumble. I don't see any tears, though, so I really think you're going to be okay."

Will squeezed his eyes shut in an effort to produce a teardrop.

A smile softened Sam's face. "Did you take your dog for a walk? Where did you go?"

The eyes popped open, still dry. "The park." He pointed down the street, then giggled when the dog nuzzled his ear. "Hawshey licked my ear."

"I think he's happy that you stopped crying," Sam said.

AJ stood and took his son's hand. The dog, apparently satisfied that his young master was okay, strained on his leash and tried to get in the front door. The floor of the foyer was covered with a tarp, and an industrial vacuum and a stepladder sat in the middle of the room. "We didn't mean to interrupt your work. Come on, Will. We'll put Hershey in the backyard and see what Annie has made for a snack."

"Cookies!"

Sam stood, too. "Or maybe an apple and some carrot sticks. I saw her cutting them up a while ago."

Will's vigorous head-shake got his curls bouncing. "Cookies!"

The warmth in her eyes evaporated when she shifted her gaze from Will to him. "The walls are sanded and primed and I'm ready to start painting. Kristi said to let you know when the first coat is on so you can make sure the color's okay."

"Whatever she's chosen, I'm sure it'll be fine." He helped his son put his mitten back on and took his hand. "Let's go, Will. Hershey, come on." He glanced back at Sam as the dog bounded down the steps. "I guess maybe I'll see you…ah…a little later."

At the corner of the house, he glanced back at the porch in time to see Sam grab the handle of the paint can and haul it inside. Her strength had always impressed him, even before he'd seen her stripped of the work clothes, and he remembered all too well the results of the hard, physical work she did—a stunning, well-toned body that could fire a man's lust in ways he'd never imagined. And once he'd had her, he hadn't been able to get enough of her.

He opened the gate for Will and let the dog off the

leash. After the pair disappeared around the back of the house, he shut the gate and waited, struggling to regain his composure. Sam would have looked beautiful when she was pregnant, and he wished he'd been able to run his hands over that firm, full belly and feel his baby growing inside her. He still couldn't believe she had denied him the opportunity, would never forgive her for wanting to get rid of their son. But he still lusted for her, and he hated that even more. If every encounter with her was going to dredge up these old emotions, he would have to do a better job of steering clear of her.

SAM SCREWED THE LONG handle on to her roller, dipped the roller into the paint tray and started applying the rich beige color Kristi had chosen to the walls. She wished she was doing something that required her full concentration instead of a mindless task like painting. She didn't want to think about AJ's tender inspection of poor little Will's hands and face after he tripped on the steps. She didn't want to remember the way her heart had practically gone into arrest when she hadn't been able to prevent his fall. She didn't want to speculate how Will had acquired those gentle brown eyes. Until she figured out a plan for finding out whose child he really was, she needed to keep her mind on other things or she'd make herself crazy.

After a couple of minutes, she lowered the roller and took a good long look at the wall. Was this really beige? It looked more like pink, at least in this light. She checked the paint pail.

The color code and the word *Bisque* had been written on the lid in black marker.

Bisque sounded beige, but for all she knew, it could be pink. She would do almost anything to avoid another encounter with AJ, but there was no point in painting the whole foyer if this wasn't the color Kristi wanted. Damn. She set the roller on the tray, propped the handle against the wall, and reluctantly made her way into the kitchen.

When she got there, she should have felt relieved to find Annie Dobson supervising the little boy's snack time and Kristi on her hands and knees, emptying the cupboard under the sink, but no sign of AJ. Instead of being relieved, she wondered where he was.

"Sam-I-am!" William waved a chunk of apple at her. "I having a snack."

The nanny beamed at her. "Hello, dear. Would you like to join us?"

"Thanks, but no. I just have a question for—"

"Ouch!" Kristi banged her head on the cupboard as she backed out, muttering something that sounded mildly profane but quiet enough not to be heard by innocent young ears. "Man, there must be twenty-five years' worth of half-used cleaning products and dried-up old sponges under here." When her face came into view, it was streaked with grime and she sported an ear-to-ear smile. "What's up?"

Sam grinned back. "I hate to interrupt that, but I think you should take a look at the paint before I get too far with it."

"What's the problem?"

"It looks awfully pink."

Kristi washed her hands under the kitchen faucet and dried them on a towel. "The color I chose should be a little on the pink side but not 'awfully' pink. Let's take a look." On the way out of the room, she linked her arm through Sam's. "AJ dropped the kid off in the kitchen a while ago and beat a hasty retreat upstairs. Are the two of you avoiding each other?"

"Shhh." Sam glanced back over her shoulder. "What if someone hears you?"

Kristi laughed. "I'm pretty sure Annie's wondering the same thing, and AJ won't hear anything, holed up in his bedroom. He told her he'd be working up there today so he won't be in your way."

"You mean 'our' way."

"Just yours, according to him."

"Good." And she wished she meant it because AJ wanting to avoid her could only be a good thing. "Let's hope he does stay out of my way."

"He also said he's behind on a deadline. Probably because he spent yesterday afternoon watching you."

"How did you know that's what he was doing?"

Kristi laughed. "How did you *not* know that's what he was doing? He was watching you from an upstairs window when I got here and he never took his eyes off you all day."

That wasn't entirely true. He had disappeared for a while because he hadn't been watching her when Will tried to get out of the house. Even though their brief run-in on the porch this morning didn't get physical the way yesterday's kitchen encounter had, it had *felt* physical. Kneeling there next to him, making sure Will hadn't hurt himself and then—heaven help her—the gentle way he'd touched his son's forehead had made her desperately want him to touch her, too.

So, yeah, it bugged the hell out of her that he would not want to be in the same room with her. Not because she wanted him here—he was too damn distracting— but she wanted *him* to want to be here.

But all of this was a waste of time, and she had work

to do. "What do you think of the paint? Is this the color you had in mind?"

Kristi stood back and studied the strip of wall Sam had already painted. "Yes, I love it, and I wouldn't call it pink at all. More like warm beige."

Sam couldn't help rolling her eyes.

"Hey, I saw that," Kristi said. "This color's perfect with all this woodwork. Not too much contrast, and it works well with the white ceilings. We'll use it throughout the main floor, except in the kitchen and powder room. I'd like those spaces to be a little brighter."

Sam grabbed her roller and dipped it in the tray. "Then I'll get back to work."

"Me, too. Come and get me when the first coat is done. I'd like to see it. Oh, and we're invited to have lunch in the kitchen."

"Oh. I thought Claire was bringing sushi?"

Kristi shook her head. "She called to say she's busy with a client and won't be able to make it."

Great. Because of the promise of sushi, Sam hadn't brought lunch today.

"AJ won't be joining us, if that's what you're worried about," Kristi said, as though she'd suddenly become a mind reader. "I heard Annie say she'd take his lunch to him upstairs so he could keep working."

Sam wondered if Will would eat upstairs with his father or in the kitchen with them, but she couldn't bring herself to ask. "I'll think about it." If it was just the two of them and the nanny, maybe there'd be an opportunity to ask a casual question or two about Will's birthday or, better yet, the whereabouts of Will's mother.

"Good. I'll check back with you at lunchtime and twist your arm." Kristi hugged her and went back to the kitchen.

Sam dug her iPod out of her jacket pocket, plugged her earphones into her ears and cranked the volume, hoping to crowd all those questions out of her mind. It must have worked because the rest of the morning flew by and by lunchtime she had finished cutting in the corners when Kristi appeared.

"*Our client* is definitely having lunch upstairs. The little guy has already eaten and the nanny's taking him shopping for new shoes, so we have the kitchen all to ourselves. She left us each a roast beef sandwich, and there's a plate of the most incredible-looking brownies I've ever seen."

Sam's mouth was already watering. Roast beef made the possibility of running into AJ almost worth the risk. "I don't know—"

Kristi grabbed her arm and pulled her toward the back of the house. "If he does show up, I'll protect you. You don't have a thing to worry about."

The hell she didn't. If AJ did show up, Kristi was more likely to make up an excuse to leave them alone, but Sam allowed herself to be led into the kitchen anyway. Sure enough, there was no sign of AJ, and the food on the table looked like something she'd expect to be served in a restaurant. Each plate was garnished with sliced dill pickles and a mound of potato chips. Sam sat down and Kristi joined her across the table.

Sam bit into her roast beef sandwich and nodded appreciatively. The tang of mustard tickled her taste buds, the lettuce was crisp and the bread wasn't just fresh, it was fresh-baked.

"Glad you changed your mind?"

"Mmm-hmm." After her second mouthful had been savored and swallowed, she set the sandwich down, poured herself a glass of ice water and took a look around the kitchen. Three labeled plastic bins and two cardboard boxes were stacked beside the fridge. "You've had a busy morning."

"I sure have. This kitchen has loads of storage space, and every square inch was packed full of stuff. Some of it's pretty cool, too. I don't think Mrs. Harris ever threw anything away."

"What did you find this morning?" Sam asked.

"Two boxes of old mason jars. Those are being donated to a thrift store. One of the bins is full of china cups and saucers, and the other two are filled with baking equipment. Annie's going to keep the cups and I'm glad because some of them are really pretty and I'd never find a better home for them."

Sam thought of the meager collection her mother used when she "entertained" royalty. Not that she would ever want anything from this house, and it was too late now, anyway.

"The consignment stores that specialize in vintage kitchenware will take the things in the other two bins for sure."

Had Annie remembered to look for cookie sheets and an extra rolling pin? Sam didn't want to ask, but before she left for the day she would remind her about the gingerbread recipe. "Have you talked to Claire this morning?" she asked.

"Just for a few minutes. She and Marlie are going over the accounts and sending out the month-end invoices today. She said to call if we need anything."

"I'm good," Sam said. "I painted the foyer ceiling yesterday. Today I'll finish painting the walls and install the new light fixture, and that room will be finished."

"Wow. You're really moving."

And the sooner she was out of here, the better. "Any

chance we can get the artwork and all those knick-knacks out of the living room this afternoon? I'd like to strip that wallpaper tomorrow."

"Sure. Will you be able to give me a hand? I have to leave a little earlier than usual, though. Jenna has an appointment with the orthodontist after school today."

"No problem," she said. "I have to pick up some light fixtures but that won't take long." She would call Mrs. Stanton after lunch and ask her to warm up last night's leftover pasta for Tildy. It meant staying late to finish the foyer and although she would rather not, she reminded herself for the umpteenth time that the more she accomplished now, the sooner she'd be out of here forever. She thought of Will trying to squeeze out a tear after he fell this morning and all the what-ifs she'd been asking rushed through her head again. The big question now…did she really want to be out of their lives forever?

Chapter Nine

With Will distracted by a small bowl of vanilla ice cream and a gingerbread cookie after dinner, AJ helped Annie clear away the dinner dishes. During the meal his son had talked endlessly about his latest fascination... the woman he insisted on calling "Sam-I-am." He chattered about her truck, he wanted a pair of work boots like hers, and during dinner he reinvented his cutlery as a hammer, saw and screwdriver.

AJ hadn't known how to shift the conversation to another topic, and it hadn't helped that Annie seemed to encourage his son's interest in Sam's work. At least Will was blissfully unaware that, at that very moment, Sam was still at work in the foyer. That was something to be thankful for.

Will's spoon clanked into his bowl. "All done."

Annie added his dishes to the load in the dishwasher. "Then it must be bath time."

"Boat time!"

She ruffled Will's curls. "That, too. Unless your father would rather get you ready for bed."

"Not bed. Boats!"

"I'd better take Hershey out before bedtime. You go

have a bath with your boats and I'll be up in a while to read you a story."

"Green Eggs an' Ham!"

Annie chuckled as she lifted him out of his seat. Will's feet were running before they hit the floor. "Is that what you want for breakfast?" she asked, following him up the back stairs. "Green eggs and ham?"

He couldn't quite hear Will's muffled response but he imagined it had something to do with Sam.

Ten minutes later, after Hershey's evening romp around the backyard, he came back inside and settled the dog into his crate for the night. The house was silent, which was good because it meant Sam had left for the evening, the house was his again and he could finally relax. He'd managed to steer clear of her since Will's tumble on the front porch that morning. Avoidance was a good strategy, one he planned to stick to for the next few weeks. Now that she was gone, though, he would take a quick look to see what she and Kristi had accomplished that day. Then he'd head on up the front staircase and get his son settled in for the night.

He knew progress was being made in the foyer, but to his surprise the living room had also been cleared of half a century's worth of Grandmother Harris's keepsakes, and the scent of dust and furniture polish lingered in the air. The furniture had been shoved into the middle of the room and covered with white sheets, and stacks of Kristi's now-familiar blue plastic bins were piled by the door, filled, he was sure, with doilies and knickknacks. The faded wallpaper, with its numerous dark squares and rectangles where artwork and framed family portraits had for decades adorned the walls, was a stark reminder that the comfortable life he'd become accustomed to would soon be behind him.

Talk about maudlin. And it wasn't even true, he reminded himself. The cabin in Idaho was a little on the
rustic side, but it was cozy and comfortable, with plenty
of room for him and a small boy and a growing dog. The
very cabin that just days ago had offered the promise
of a fresh new start, far away from people who might
unravel the tightly woven fabric of his life. People like
Sam. It had been only a few days since she'd come
crashing back into his life, but it already felt like an
eternity. Grandmother Harris would have been quick to
remind him that's what living a lie did to a person. The
lie, at least this particular one, would be behind him in
a couple of weeks, though. The house would be staged
and on the market, and he and Will and Hershey would
be settled in Idaho in time for Christmas.

He circled the mountain of furniture and crossed the
living room to the French doors that led to the foyer to
see if that room was finished. The doors were open,
and what he got was an eyeful of Sam's rear end.

She was standing on a stepladder with her back to
him, and that luscious blue-jean-clad backside was at
eye level. She was installing a new ceiling light fixture,
and with her arms extended overhead, her T-shirt had
ridden up, exposing a strip of soft, smooth skin that
begged to be touched.

Get the hell out of here, he told himself. But he
couldn't move. He let his gaze travel up her back and
her slender arms, and he watched her twist electrical
wires with a pair of pliers. Her arms, sculpted by work
that was traditionally done by a man, were startlingly
feminine. Downright sexy, even. He'd always been impressed that she knew how to do these things, and it
bugged the hell out of him that she still turned him on
the way no other woman ever had.

The room was illuminated by a single lightbulb in a wire cage, angled so she could see what she was doing. The harsh light also sharpened her profile, emphasizing her striking beauty and cool detachment. She had earbuds in her ears, and the accompanying white wire snaked around her slender waist and disappeared into one back pocket. The ladder wobbled as she dropped one arm, then steadied again when she tucked the pliers into the other pocket and plucked a small orange cap from between her teeth. She started to twist it on to the wires she was working with, but it slipped out of her fingers.

Instinctively they both reached for it, and that's when she noticed him.

The ladder swayed and she let out a startled gasp.

He didn't remember seeing her fall, didn't realize he'd leaped forward, but he was acutely aware of her body once she was in his arms. She was solid muscle and heavier than she looked, but he hooked an arm beneath her knees and braced himself with a backward step so they didn't end up in a heap on the floor.

Her soft brown eyes, the one feature that hinted she had a gentler side, were now dark and her glare was frosty. She pulled the earphone out of one ear. "You scared the hell out of me. How long were you standing there?"

"Sorry." He didn't answer her question because he didn't know the answer. Time always seemed to stand still, or at least slow to a snail's pace, when he watched her.

"I need you to put me down." Her arms were wound snugly around his neck, though, and her lush full lips, only inches from his, parted slightly. Both actions suggested she needed something entirely different.

He damn well knew better than to point that out. He also knew better than to *show* her what she needed, what they both needed, but that wasn't going to stop him. Although she'd betrayed him in a way no other woman ever could, the soft scent of her hair and the heat from her body against his flowed through his veins like a drug he couldn't get enough of.

He kissed her hungrily, his own need easily outstripping hers.

Sam's arms tightened around his neck, and then her tongue touched his and he was done for. Nothing mattered now except that each of them had a need that only the other could meet.

Seconds later—or maybe minutes, he had no idea—Sam was getting heavier and he had a stitch in his side. With his mouth pressed to hers, their breaths mingling, he lowered her feet to the floor. She tried to move away but he kept her close, and she let him.

Time went into limbo again. He slid one hand down her back until it encountered the pliers in her pocket. On the way back up, he slipped his fingers under her T-shirt. The feel of her warm skin made him want to touch more of her, all of her.

The skin-to-skin contact seemed to have the opposite effect on Sam, or at least she was the first to come to her senses. She yanked her arms away, grabbed his shoulders and shoved. "You shouldn't have done that."

He didn't know if she meant the kiss or his hand beneath her shirt. Probably both. But the way she'd parted her lips for him, subconscious or not, she wasn't fooling him. "You didn't want me to kiss you?"

"Yes. No." She shook her head. "I *didn't* want you to."

"Then why did you kiss me back?"

She took a couple of steps away. "I didn't."

With smug satisfaction, he took in the rapid rise and fall of her chest. "You're lying."

"I didn't *want* to kiss you."

"Could have fooled me. But then, you always could."

Her color rose. She yanked the remaining earpiece from her ear, pulled a wafer-thin device from her back pocket and wound the wire around it. "Go to hell," she said, and grabbed her shirt from where she'd tossed it over a toolbox. "I'm the one who got fooled, or have you forgotten…?" She hesitated, as though her train of thought had been interrupted. Then the rest of what she had to say came out in a rush. "You were already married to someone else, and when you were finished with me, you didn't have the balls to break it off. You had your father threaten me instead."

A slap on the face would have startled him less. His father had *threatened* her? What the hell? The past flashed through his mind as he struggled to remember everything he'd tried so hard to forget.

"My father spoke to you?" A heavy mass settled in AJ's gut.

Sam shoved her arms into the shirt, drew it closed and fastened it with crossed arms. It was a stance he knew too well, one that told him she was pulling away, withdrawing into her silent self.

"Don't play games." She practically spat the words at him.

He wanted to ask what the old man had said to her. Even more, he wanted to know what she had said to him. He also knew she would never tell him. Besides, he reminded himself, he was venturing into dangerous territory. Regardless of what had transpired between the father he despised and the woman he had once loved, he couldn't risk exposing his own secret. William was everything and he didn't dare lose sight of that. Safer to back off and acknowledge one defeat than to make demands and risk losing everything.

If she wanted to believe he'd sent his father to break up with her, then he would go along with it. "What I did was wrong," he said. "I should have talked to you myself."

He watched for her reaction, but she wasn't giving anything away.

"And I apologize for kissing you just now," he said. "I was out of line."

She was still wary, but she no longer looked like a rabbit ready to bolt. "You caught me off guard and I wasn't expecting—" She stopped and glanced past him. "Annie. Hi."

AJ turned around and encountered Annie's wide smile and the all-knowing sparkle in her eyes. Seriously? Could her timing be any worse?

"So sorry to interrupt—" Her smiled widened, and there was no apology in it. "When I realized Sam was still here, I thought I'd better give her these baking supplies." The handle of a rolling pin protruded from the box she carried. "The gingerbread recipe is in here, too."

"Thank you," Sam said. "I appreciate you giving these things to me. I mean—" she flicked her gaze at AJ "—lending them to me. I'll return them."

He shoved his hands in his pockets. "Keep them. Please."

Annie set the box on the floor. "You're welcome to keep them, otherwise Kristi will donate them to a thrift store. Now...I'll just leave the two of you to get back to whatever you were doing before I interrupted."

She finished off that sassy comment with another wide sparkling smile. "William's waiting for you upstairs. I'll go up and keep an eye on him till you're free." With that, she turned around and ambled off to the kitchen.

For a dedicated, hardworking employee, she could be downright infuriating.

Sam was looking at the box Annie had given her like a kid who'd been caught with her hand in the cookie jar. "I only asked for the recipe. She wanted to know if I had all the equipment I needed and I said I didn't think so and she said I could borrow some but I didn't plan to keep them." She paused for a breath. "Sorry. We should have asked first."

"My grandmother had enough to equip several kitchens. You're welcome to take anything you'd like."

She shook her head. "I'll return it."

"That's up to you." He didn't want to talk about rolling pins and cookie sheets, and he wished this wasn't making her so uncomfortable. From what he could see, Annie had assembled a box of odds and ends that would never be missed, at least not by him.

Sam pulled the pliers from her back pocket and motioned to the light fixture dangling from the ceiling. "It's late. Your son is waiting for you, and I should finish this and get home to my...home."

She was right. He'd promised Will he'd be up to say good-night. As he climbed the stairs, though, he found himself wondering what she'd meant to say before she replaced it with the word *home*.

SAM LET HERSELF INTO THE apartment and was greeted by the familiar sound of the television. For once, instead of resenting her mother's predictable routine, she welcomed it. There were no surprises.

"Mom? I'm home." She set the box of baking supplies on the floor and dumped her other things on the rickety hall table, then sat down to unlace her work boots.

"*Dancing with the Stars* is on," Tildy said.

Sam put her boots and jacket away in the closet. She was exhausted and yet her body hummed with pent-up energy, compliments of AJ Harris and his pleasure-inducing hands and the searing-hot kisses that left her boneless with desire. Now she hoped the son of a bitch was feeling exactly the same way, only more turned on. And guilty. Guilty for what he'd done to her then and for what he'd done to her tonight...but mostly because he got to sit with William and read him a story and tuck him into bed.

"I had dinner," Tildy called from the living room. "Mrs. Stanton brought fried chicken."

"Sounds delicious, Mom. I'll be sure to thank her," she said, even though she had already checked with her to find out if her mother had eaten that day.

Sam picked up the box and carried it into the tiny galley kitchen, grateful to see her mother's dinner dishes had been washed and set in the rack to drip dry. Mrs. Stanton really was a treasure.

There was another completed jigsaw puzzle on the kitchen table, and in the living room her mother sat in her usual place on the sofa, wearing the bathrobe and slippers she'd had on that morning. Sam sat next to her and gave her a hug, as she always did. "How are you feeling today, Mom?"

Tildy, remote in hand, changed channels without looking away from the screen. "A little tired."

"Did you have any visitors today?"

"Mrs. Stanton. She came for lunch and again for dinner."

"That was nice of her."

"I don't mind the company, but you'd think she'd stay home once in a while and feed that husband of hers."

For a couple of seconds, Sam pressed her lips together in case her mother caught her smiling. "She likes spending time with you," she said once she had herself under control. "And I'm sure she feeds him, too."

Sam had never understood why her mother didn't like being taken care of when she never lifted a finger to help herself, but she'd learned long ago to play up Mrs. Stanton's "visits" and downplay the part about being helped.

"She said you had to work late."

"I did, sorry about that." She covered her mother's hand with her own, noting, as always, the cool, papery skin covering bone and not much else. "I'm not working on Saturday, and I thought if might be fun to bake cookies."

Tildy looked away from the television and actually directed her gaze right at Sam's. "What kind of cookies?"

Sam looked into her mother's pale blue-gray eyes and soaked up the attention. "Gingerbread. They'll be nice for Christmas."

"I'd like that." Tildy didn't say anything else. She didn't have to. Those precious few seconds of eye contact were worth a thousand "I love you's."

"So, it was just you and Mrs. Stanton today? Any other visitors?"

"Just the two of us."

A day without delusions was a positive sign, but Sam knew better than to get her hopes up. In the past she'd let herself get caught up in wishful thinking, and then had her hopes dashed when her mother took a turn for the worse. This time the doctor had warned that her mother might feel tired and have no appetite, but there was a chance the delusions would persist. Still, a good day was a good day.

"Can I get you anything before I have a shower?" She needed to make herself something to eat, too, since Annie had made lunch for her and Kristi today.

"A cup of tea would be nice."

"I'll plug in the kettle now and make tea when I'm out of the shower."

Her mother's attention was back on the television, though, and she didn't reply.

Sam filled the kettle, set it to boil and went into her bedroom. The first thing to catch her attention was the overflowing laundry hamper.

At AJ's, the washer and drier were conveniently located in the pantry off the kitchen, and in the short time Sam had been there, she'd noticed Annie often had the washer or drier running while she was busy in the kitchen. If Ready Set Sold took off to the point where Sam earned enough money to pay her mother's medical bills *and* rent a nicer apartment, maybe even buy a condo, in-suite laundry would be at the top of her wish list. She shoved the hamper deeper into the closet and closed the door. Out of sight, out of mind, for tonight at least.

An hour later, after she'd showered, nibbled at a sandwich and coaxed her mother to turn off the television and turn in for the night, she set the box of baking supplies on the counter and peered inside. She felt like a kid on Christmas morning. Along with the cookie sheet, two of them it turned out, and the rolling pin, there was a large mixing bowl, four nested measuring cups, a well-worn wooden spatula and an old set of metal measuring spoons on a loop of red ribbon, one with a bent handle.

The last things in the box were a recipe card for Holiday Gingerbread, and a cookie cutter in the shape of a gingerbread man. Had Annie given her the cookie cutter that she and Will had used to make theirs? She took them out of the box and ran a fingertip over Annie's neatly written script as she perused the ingredients and then the instructions, and then she took a closer look at the cookie cutter. It was new, with a department-store tag still attached, along with a note in the same tight handwriting as the recipe card.

Dear Samantha,
Have fun baking cookies with your mother. The recipe also includes instructions for making a gingerbread house, in case you'd like to build yourself a home for the holidays. Merry Christmas!
Annie.

Sam swiped at her eyes with the sleeve of her sweatshirt and reread the note. A gingerbread house seemed a tad ambitious for someone who'd never in her life baked cookies, but she would see how her mother was feeling on Saturday. She knew better than to let herself imagine that decorating gingerbread men with her would be as much fun as Annie and Will had been having, but Tildy had had a pretty good day today. Practically normal, and Sam could use a little normal right now.

She yawned. She could also use some sleep. After she tucked away her new treasures—everything except the recipe card and cookie cutter—in an almost-empty bottom cupboard, she carried the recipe and the cookie cutter with Annie's note to her bedroom, set them on the dresser beside her bed and crawled under the covers. An hour later, she was still wide-awake, unable to chase away images of little brown-eyed Will laughing and calling her Sam-I-am, and of being caught in AJ's dark blue gaze right before he kissed her. She was in for a long night and her only consolation was the hope that he was in exactly the same place she was.

Before tonight she wouldn't have been so sure, but that kiss…

Would he have kissed her if he didn't still have feelings for her? Had he ever had feelings for her? The answer to those questions lay in finding out the identity of Will's mother, and she needed to figure out a way to do that. Beneath that "tall, dark and tortured" exterior, AJ Harris was a family man. He wasn't just a good father, he was heart-wrenchingly gentle with William, and so patient. Devoted in ways so many men weren't. Her own father, for example. Kristi's deadbeat ex-husband, for another.

During her brief affair with AJ, she'd been convinced he was in love with her, even though he'd never said he was. If he hadn't been in love with her, he was still attracted to her now. As for her feelings, she wasn't over him, either. The only difference between then and now was that they'd each had a child. Possibly just one child, one impossibly adorable little boy who somehow had her father's eyes.

Still, she reminded herself, AJ had tried his damnedest to sound surprised earlier tonight when she'd brought up James Harris's conversation with her. She hadn't bought it for a minute. She'd wanted to throw something at him, make a dent in that aristocratic forehead with a pair of pliers. She'd also wanted to scream at him and demand to know who William's mother was. The past was the past, and although she'd given up their child, he'd had no right to take him, if that's what he'd done. If he had, she had every bit as much right to lay claim to the child, too. That had not been part of the adoption agreement she'd signed, and she never would have signed it if it had.

Life didn't offer a redo, but if there was a chance she could have her son back in her life, she intended to take it.

AJ POURED TWO FINGERS of Scotch into a crystal high-ball and returned the bottle to its top-shelf home in the pantry. If an hour of tossing and turning hadn't resulted in sleep, maybe this would. He wandered through the dark, silent house and ended up in the foyer before he realized where he was going.

For the first time since his unexpected encounter with Sam earlier in the evening, he took a good look around. She had accomplished a lot in two days, but then he'd seen her work before so this was no surprise. Before she left, she had finished installing the ceiling light—a rectangular copper fixture with two suspended, stained-glass shades. He flicked the switch and, as it illuminated the room, recalled the discussion the day she and her partners had toured the house, and realized they'd been right. This one worked better.

A five-gallon pail of paint stood by the front door, with several neatly folded drop cloths piled on top. Next to that the folded stepladder leaned against the wall, and next to that sat Sam's toolbox. He found himself wanting to open it, though for the life of him he didn't know why. He opened it anyway.

Her tools were arranged neatly in compartments, much the way she organized her life. After she stopped seeing him, he had realized how little he knew about her. She was quiet and reserved without being a wall-flower, meticulous about her work, looked like a god-dess behind closed doors and made love like a woman whose sole purpose in life was to please and be pleased. Out of habit he hadn't shared many details about his family background. She shared even fewer.

Against Melanie Morrow's advice, he had gone to Sam's apartment after discovering she might be having his baby, knowing she would never answer if he called. She wasn't home the day he dropped by unannounced, but her mother, Tildy, had happily let him in. She'd been wearing the kind of dress a woman might have worn to a cocktail party in the sixties, ruby-red satin, as he recalled, with heavy, badly applied makeup. She in-vited him in for tea, although none was served, insisted on calling him Prince Andrew and regaled him with stories about other and equally famous guests she had entertained. When asked about Sam, she acknowledged that her daughter was pregnant, she didn't know who the father was and Sam had hired a lawyer to arrange a private adoption because babies were noisy and they had no place for it to sleep. Sam had relegated their son to one of her life's compartments as easily as she arranged everything else.

AJ slammed her toolbox shut, stood and flexed his knees. He sipped the Scotch, hoping the drink would wash away the taste of her. He regretted kissing her, but then he was no stranger to regret. If she hadn't fallen, ended up in his arms, he never would have touched her. Now that he had, he wanted her more than ever. Or maybe he just needed a woman. He knew that wasn't the case, though. He'd tried that after she'd broken things off with him. It hadn't helped him get over her, but it had been one more thing to add to a growing list of regrets.

The biggest shock tonight was finding out that his father had talked to her. He had no idea what the old man had said to her, but he had somehow convinced her that AJ no longer wanted anything to do with her. Had his father known about the baby all along? AJ found that hard to believe, but there was only one way to find out.

Chapter Ten

First thing the next morning, Sam filled the wallpaper steamer from a hose at the side of the house, and hauled it up the front steps and into the living room. If she never saw another wallpapered wall in her life, she would be a happy woman. A wet nose nudged her arm as she plugged in the machine.

"Good dog." She gave Hershey a pat on the head, expecting someone to show up and retrieve him and hoping that someone wouldn't be AJ, but no one did.

The oversize puppy opened his mouth into a doggie smile, tongue extended, and most of the rest of him started to wag.

Sam laughed. As much as she wanted to avoid AJ, she couldn't work with an energetic pup in the way. "Come on, boy. Let's go find your people." The dog happily followed her to the kitchen.

Will was perched in a booster seat at the kitchen table, eating oatmeal. Annie was sliding two loaves of bread into the oven. "Good morning, Sam," she said after she straightened and turned around. "Oh, dear. Was that rascal getting in your way?"

"Not yet, but I'll be taking down more wallpaper

this morning and it might be best to keep him out of the living room."

"Hershey, here, boy. Out you go, run off a little steam." Annie opened the back door and the dog bolted into the yard.

Will stuck his spoon into the remains of his oatmeal. "Hawshey wants to play. I go play, too."

"Not in your pajamas. Finish your breakfast and you can play with Hershey after you get dressed." The nanny pulled a tissue from the pocket of her apron and wiped a dribble of milk from the boy's chin. "Can I get you some coffee?" she asked Sam. "You look a little tired this morning."

She was tired. Make that exhausted. Dragging herself out of bed this morning hadn't been easy, yet out of habit she had dressed, laced on her running shoes and gone out for an early-morning run. She hadn't run as hard as she had the day before, or as far, but she'd needed "her fix," as Kristi called it.

Coming home to the quiet, dark apartment felt like crawling into a cocoon and she'd been tempted to stay there, catch up on laundry, shop for the ingredients she needed for the cookies, spend some time with her mother. Kristi and Claire would have understood. She could easily make up one day and stay on schedule.

Then she'd asked herself, *what would AJ think?* That he'd been able to intimidate her, again? That she was trying to avoid him? He'd be right on the second count, but no way would she give him the satisfaction of thinking she stayed home because of him.

"I'd love a cup of coffee, as long as you don't mind if I take it into the living room and have it while I work."

"I don't mind at all." Annie poured the coffee and set it on the table along with a sugar bowl and creamer shaped like tomatoes. "Unless you'd like to sit for a bit and have a muffin."

If it was one of the muffins she'd had the other day, she'd love one, but she did not want to be sitting here when AJ came downstairs.

"Mr. Harris is out today," Annie said.

The woman could easily pass herself off as a mind reader.

Annie took a muffin out of a tin, set it on a plate and popped it into the microwave. "He has some business to take care of. Have a seat. Would you like butter with this?"

Sam sat and nodded in response to butter.

Annie took the butter out of the fridge, the microwave pinged, and before Sam could say "chocolate-banana muffin," she'd whisked the plate onto the table next to Sam's coffee cup. "There you go. William, finish your cereal. Oatmeal makes little boys grow up to be big and strong."

"Thank you," Sam said.

"I am big." As he had the other day, Will used his arms to demonstrate how big.

"You're welcome, Sam. Don't you want to be big enough to reach the top of your bookshelf, William?"

Will nodded and eagerly spooned another mound of oatmeal into his mouth.

Annie smiled. "That's my boy."

She certainly had a way with children. *Would I have this much patience and imagination if I were a mother?* Sam wondered.

"I'll be sure to keep young William and that rowdy dog out of your way while Mr. Harris is out."

"Oh. Um, thanks," Sam said, smiling at the woman's ability to serve food and carry on two conversations.

"And thank you very much for the recipe. We…my mom and I…will make the cookies for sure. I'm not sure I'm ready to tackle a gingerbread house, though."

"I have a gingerbread man?" Will asked.

"Not for breakfast," Annie said. "It's a tried-and-true recipe I've been using for years. You'll have to let me know how yours turn out."

"I will. My mom and I don't do a lot of Christmassy things, so it should be fun." She hoped.

"Does your mother work?"

"No. She hasn't really been well since I was a kid."

"And your father?"

"He and my mom split up when I was a teenager, so he wasn't around much, then he died a couple of years ago."

"I'm sorry to hear that. It must be hard."

Sam was sorry, too. Every month her father had given them a couple hundred dollars, which had helped with her mother's meds, but he hadn't had life insurance and after his bills were paid, there'd been no money left. "We get by," Sam said.

"What sort of health problems does your mother have?"

She wasn't in the habit of sharing this kind of information with strangers, but something about the woman made Sam want to confide in her. Still, she hesitated.

"Mental illness?" Annie asked.

"Yes. How could you tell?"

"If she had a bad heart, you wouldn't have been reluctant to tell me."

Smart woman. "I guess you're right. Most people don't understand that it's a real medical problem, they just think she's crazy."

Annie's eyes were filled with genuine sympathy.

"Over the years I've worked with a lot of patients who suffer from various forms of mental illness or Alzheimer's. That's why Mr. Harris hired me. The old lady was in the early stages of dementia when her heart gave out."

She wondered how long AJ and Will had lived here before Annie joined them. Since Will was born? She watched the child now, all of his attention focused on finishing his breakfast, and tried to ignore the ache in her chest. Had AJ lived here with Will's mother? If so, it was strange no one ever mentioned her. It was almost as if the child didn't have a mother. Sam still couldn't wrap her head around the coincidence of Will's birthday. She wanted to ask Annie, but couldn't find the right words. "I'm sorry about Mrs. Harris," she said instead. "It sounds as though you were fond of her."

"She was a lovely woman. Thought the sun rose and set on that grandson of hers. And young William, well, in her eyes a more perfect child had never been born."

A perfect child who was at that moment using dribbled milk to finger-paint the place mat under his bowl. Annie chuckled as she rinsed a washcloth with warm water and used it to wipe his hands and face before she lifted him out of his booster seat and set him on the floor. "I'll sure miss them when they're gone to Idaho."

"You're not going with them?"

"No. I'm not fond of the mountains and especially not the snow. Seattle winters are plenty cold enough for me. Besides, it's a small house compared to this one and Mr. Harris won't need me there."

"I'm sure you won't have trouble finding another position here in the city." AJ was as fond of her as she was of him, and would no doubt give her a glowing recommendation.

"What about you, dear? Have you thought about hiring someone to help with your mother?"

Almost daily. "I have a neighbor who looks in on her during the day and makes sure she has something to eat. She won't accept any money, but I do pay her for the groceries. My mom's medications are pretty expensive, so I'm afraid that's about all I can afford."

Annie patted her hand. "Things have a way of working themselves out, and I have a good feeling about you."

Sam would love to believe that things would work out, and she had no trouble imagining a better life, but in reality, things were as good as they were going to get until she started to earn more money. And she wondered if Annie's "good feeling" might stem from her walking in on Sam and AJ last night.

"Hawshey wants in!" Will and his dog stood nose to nose on either side of the glass door that led to the backyard. The boy's excited shrieks matched the dog's vigorous tail-wagging.

Annie opened the door and the dog bounded into the kitchen. "Oh, no, you don't," she said, grabbing the dog's collar and reaching for an old towel. "Those wet paws will make a big mess of my nice clean floors."

Sam could see the dog was too much for the nanny to manage, so she quickly got up and offered to help.

Annie gratefully relinquished the towel. "Thank you. Mr. Harris usually takes these two for a walk after breakfast so they can run off some steam."

"To the park!" Will shouted, jumping up and down.

The dog joined in while Sam did her best to dry off his oversize paws. "Maybe when your dad gets home," she said.

Annie sighed. "He'll be out all day, I'm afraid."

"Park, park, park!"

"William, no shouting in the house. We'll have to find something quiet to do indoors today."

Good luck with that. The boy and his dog were feeding off one another's energy and getting more wound up by the minute.

"How far is it to the park?" Sam asked.

"Two blocks."

She really should tackle that wallpaper, but since Annie had been so kind to her, she felt she owed her a favor in return. "I guess I could take them for half an hour or so before I start to work." She held her breath, scarcely able to believe she'd just offered to take Will out on her own, and wondering what AJ would think when he found out.

"Would you, dear? These two don't do well when their routine is changed."

Sam laughed. There was an understatement. She also got the sense that if she didn't pitch in and help get their routine back on track, she wouldn't accomplish much, either.

EVEN AFTER A THREE-YEAR absence, the reception area at Harris Marketing and Communications was every bit as grand as AJ remembered. The same pretty blonde receptionist still sat behind the enormous desk wearing a headset and a smile that was every orthodontist's dream. Behind her, the company's logo—the stylized initials *H M C* forged in brass—created a focal point on the walnut paneling. Everything, including the cluster of leather club chairs, reeked of opulence. Just like the company's founder.

"Good morning, can I—?" She glanced up and her smile went narrow. "Oh. Mr. Harris. How nice to see you." Her mouth widened again, indicating she'd regained some of her composure.

"And you." For the life of him, he still couldn't remember her name. "Is the old man in?"

"Mr. Harris? Yes, I'll just buzz his secretary and—"

"Please don't. I'd like to surprise him." AJ did his best to muster a friendly smile.

"Oh." She withdrew her hand from the buttons on the switchboard. "I guess that would be okay."

They both knew James Harris didn't like surprises. The man thrived on order and control, but she seemed willing to go along with his request. He knew perfectly well that would change the instant he was out of sight.

"Thanks. I'll just head upstairs then."

He crossed the lobby and pushed the button for the elevator. While he waited, he glanced back at Ms. No-Name. She was watching him, one hand poised over the phone. He decided to take the stairs. He didn't believe for a minute that she'd refrain from giving his father's secretary a heads-up, and he could sprint up the stairs faster than the elevator could carry him to the third floor.

Sure enough, the secretary was hanging up the phone as he got there. "AJ, this is a surprise," she said, even though his appearance clearly wasn't. "Your father's on the phone, but if you'd like to take a seat—"

He was in no mood to wait, and he knew better than to think he could charm this one. "Thanks, but I'd rather not." He shoved open the double doors to his father's office and walked in unannounced.

James Harris's eyes went wide, and for a second or two he put his conversation on pause. "Ah...Bert? Sorry, something's just come up. I'll have to call you back." And without bothering to wait for a reply from

Albert Cunningham, his lifelong friend, he dropped the receiver into its cradle. "Well, well. To what do we owe this unexpected visit?"

"This isn't a social call."

"So I gather. Guests don't barge into someone's office, but you were never one to adhere to propriety."

"I'm here to talk about Sam."

His father's eyebrows knitted themselves into a phony look of puzzlement. "Sam who?"

"Samantha Elliott. The woman who believes you broke up with her on my behalf. *That* Sam."

"What about her?"

"I want to know what you said to her."

"That you found her a pleasant distraction while she worked here, but you were done with her."

His father was never one to beat around the bush but even so, AJ was momentarily stunned by the full extent of the man's interference. "For God's sake, what gave you the right to run my life?" he asked. "*Her* life?"

"I had *every* right. She's one of the have-nots, AJ. We're the haves. I needed to make sure she wasn't after your money, *our* money, so I did a little digging."

"You...what? Please tell me you didn't hire a private investigator."

"Of course I did." His father leaned back in his swivel chair but didn't say anything else. If AJ wanted to know what the investigator had discovered, his father was going to make him ask for it. Smug son of a bitch.

"And?"

"She comes from a broken home—"

AJ couldn't let that go. "So do I." He stepped closer to the desk and his father leaned back a little farther. "I've never heard you and Mom say two civil words to each other. The fact that you're still married doesn't mean our family wasn't broken."

James ignored that. "She's poor as dirt, at least she was then, and uneducated."

"Uneducated? Are you for freaking real? She built this." He gestured at the cabinets that completely covered one side wall of his father's office. "How many women, with or without a college degree, know how to do that?"

Apparently still not willing to engage in a conversation, James leaned forward again and rested his forearms on his desk, hands clasped. "I had a hunch she wasn't good enough to be a Harris, and when I checked up on her I was right."

"Nobody asked you!"

"Nobody had to. The girl's mother is as crazy as a loon. Did you know that? Between your mother and your brother, did you really think we needed more crazy in this family?"

Inside, AJ's anger roared like a caged animal. "You arrogant, self-serving bastard. You turned your back on William when he needed you most—your own son, for God's sake—and the only solution he could find on his own was to hang himself in his bedroom closet." The shock of finding his brother there still jolted him senseless every time the image flickered through his mind. "You've ignored Mom's depression but you think it's okay for her to self-medicate with booze and painkillers. It's a bloody miracle she's still alive."

His father opened his mouth to defend himself.

"I'm not finished. You have a lot of gall to look down your nose at Tildy Elliott. And FYI, she isn't 'crazy.' She's mentally ill, and it seems to me Sam does a damn good job of taking care of her. Did it ever occur to you that maybe the Harrises weren't good enough for her?"

His father was unfazed. "Are you finished now?"

"I was finished with you a long time ago. Now I'm done for good."

"Considering you're such a family man, aren't you even going to ask about your mother?"

His father's sarcasm cut like a knife. "I don't have to. I dropped by the house this morning, thinking I might catch you there."

"I see." Finally, James Harris looked a little deflated.

"I'd ask if you were going to ask about your grandson, but then *you* never were much of a family man."

AJ watched closely for his father's reaction, and was moderately appeased that he actually got one. He pulled a photograph of Will and Hershey from the inner pocket of his overcoat and tossed it on the desk. "I brought this for you, so you can see what you're missing." And then he swung around and walked out, swearing that this time it really and truly was for good.

THE TWO-BLOCK WALK TO the neighborhood park gave Sam a chance to let her excitement overcome her apprehension about being out with Will and his dog. Hershey leaped ahead on the end of his leash, but Will stayed by her side, holding her hand and jabbering nonstop. Thank goodness because this was the first time in her life she'd been alone with a young child and she had no idea how she'd manage if he was as bouncy as the dog.

Along the way, they were greeted by an elderly couple out for a morning stroll and a middle-aged man who was walking two dogs. Hershey gave the other two dogs an exuberant sniff and they reciprocated before Sam was able to tug him away.

"What do you like to do when you come to the park?" she asked when they arrived. It was a typical neighborhood park, taking up a full city block with a small playground at one end. It was quiet that morning, with no other children in sight and only an elderly couple strolling arm in arm nearby.

"Climb up and slide down."

Sam did not like the look of the climbing apparatus and the length of the giant green plastic tube that served as a slide. Way too high, she decided. No way would she risk having Will hurt himself.

"Would you like to go on the swing?" she asked. "I can push you."

Will pulled his hand out of Sam's and dashed for the swings. Relieved, she followed with Hershey and hooked the dog's leash over a post, then lifted the little boy onto the swing seat and made sure he was secure.

"Ready?" she asked.

"Ready!"

With a gentle push, he was off.

"Higher!" he shouted.

She pushed harder and he went a little higher. His laughter drifted around her while she continued to push him through the air.

"More higher!"

"You're already flying like a bird, you little daredevil." She gave him another push. "That's as high as the swing goes." Which wasn't true, but she wasn't taking any chances.

"I a bird!" Will called out, laughing as the swing rose and fell. "See, Hawshey? I a bird."

Hershey had found a stick and was happily settled on the grass, giving it a good chew.

Sam remembered pleading with her father to get a

dog, but the answer had always been no. He had enough on his hands, taking care of her and her mother. She also had vague memories of being at a park with her dad. It must have been somewhere in Seattle because they'd always lived here and had never gone anywhere for a family vacation, but she couldn't remember where they'd been living at the time. She had no idea how old she would have been, but most likely older than Will. Her father had sat on a bench, reading the paper and smoking one of the cigarettes that had ultimately taken his life, letting her do as she liked. She used to think that's what fathers did, but she had to admit AJ was nothing like that. He was as good a father as any child could wish for, and Will was a very lucky little boy.

Last night while she'd lain awake, she'd had plenty of time to contemplate her options if she found out that Will was her child, too. If she was wrong about that, and she was less and less sure she was, it would be impossible to say goodbye to him. If by some miracle he was hers and really was back in her life, AJ would have to change his plans about moving to Idaho because there was no way she would let her son go a second time. Would AJ expect her to? He could think again. She would hire a lawyer if she had to.

She had also decided she would make an appointment to see Melanie Morrow, the lawyer who handled the adoption, and confront her. Not yet, though. She would wait until she'd finished the work on AJ's house and spent more time with Will. By then she might have uncovered something more solid than a suspicion. After all, how could she be wrong when this felt so right?

"Have you had enough?" she asked, letting the swing slow and finally stop.

Will shook his head. "More."

"I think Hershey's ready to go home. Maybe he needs a dog treat or something."

"I need a treat."

"Do you? Well, let's go then. Maybe your nanny will have something ready for you when we get home." She loved the way the words *nanny* and *home* sounded as they rolled off her tongue. So domestic. *So not you,* she reminded herself. *And so completely the opposite of the reality of your life.*

She lifted Will off the swing and took his hand. Hershey, with the stick still firmly grasped between his teeth, leaped to his feet when she gathered up the leash. The walk home was uneventful and Sam congratulated herself on getting both child and dog back to the house in one piece. When she escorted her charges through the back door, Kristi was in the kitchen going over one of her lists and Annie was folding laundry on the kitchen table.

"You're back. Thank you for getting them out of my hair for a while."

Sam tucked the boy's mittens into his jacket pockets and hung it on a coat hook by the back door. The leash went on another hook, and the dog started lapping water from his bowl.

"Good morning," Kristi said, quirking her eyebrows. "I hear you went to the park."

"AJ usually takes them every morning but he's out for the day and Annie thought the morning would go more smoothly if their routine wasn't disrupted."

"Sam to the rescue. Did you have fun?" she asked Will.

"I a bird."

"Are you?" Kristi knelt beside him. "I don't see any wings."

Will flapped his arms.

"He played on the swing," Sam said.

Annie grabbed a laundry basket off the kitchen table. "Young William, you come upstairs and help me put these things away."

"What are you working on today?" Kristi asked after they left the room.

"Stripping the wallpaper out of the living room. How about you?"

"I'll tackle the dining room. All the plates and figurines on the plate rail are covered with dust. I'll take them down and Annie said she'll clean them for me. Then we'll sort the contents of the china cabinet and sideboard."

"Big job."

"I'm always curious to see what people accumulate over the years, but it's kind of sad, too. The things that had so much sentimental value for one person become somebody else's clutter. A bunch of old stuff that has to be 'dealt with.'"

Sam made a face. "That's exactly how I feel about wallpaper. If I ever have a home of my own, there won't be one scrap of wallpaper in it."

"Knowing you, there won't be any clutter in it, either. Me, on the other hand. You should see my place right now. Jenna's science fair project is spread all over the living-room carpet and I'm using the dining table as my office, so we either eat standing up in the kitchen or sitting on the sofa in the living room."

"The disorganized organizer." Sam laughed at her own joke.

Kristi joined her. "Sad, but true. Almost as soon as we moved in, I regretted buying a two-bedroom town house. A third bedroom would have made a perfect office."

Sam knew Kristi well enough to know that no matter how much space she had, she would fill it, the same way she filled a room with her energy and her ready smile. "None of the stuff you're talking about is real clutter. It's life. You'll clear off your table when this project is over, Jenna will pack up her project when the science fair is over, and everything will get back to normal."

"That's what I keep telling myself, but then that mess will just be replaced with another. That's our normal. And I didn't mention the hall closet. Boots, shoes, all the cloth grocery bags I never remember to take when I go shopping and winter coats for two humans and dog."

"Hercules has more than one coat?"

"I'm afraid so."

How many coats did one eight-pound Yorkshire terrier need? Sam knew better than to ask. Kristi and her daughter doted on that dog but even so, you'd think one coat would be enough.

Sam glanced at her watch. "Must get moving. I'm off to a late start this morning."

"I'll say. How late did you stay last night?"

Sam's face went warm. Probably red, too. "Um...I was here till seven or so."

"And you're blushing because...?" Kristi took a closer look at her face. "Hmm. Dark circles under your eyes. Did something keep you awake last night? Or someone?"

Sam's face got even warmer. "It's nothing."

"Ha. I don't believe you and I'm dying to hear all the yummy details, but we'll save those for lunch when we have more time."

"Nothing happened."

"Anything that makes our cool, calm and collected Samantha Elliott blush like a schoolgirl is a big deal." Kristi was grinning now. "And I want to hear every single detail."

"It really isn't—"

"Nuh! Do I need to call Claire? 'Cause you know if I can't wheedle it out of you, she will."

Sam knew perfectly well what would happen if the two of them ganged up on her. "Fine. We'll talk about it over lunch but I can tell you right now, you'll be disappointed." But damn it if she didn't feel herself turning red all over again.

Kristi grinned. "Sweetie, you are the world's worst liar."

That wasn't exactly true, Sam thought. She'd been living a lie for years.

Chapter Eleven

AJ drove his car onto the Bainbridge Island ferry and cut the engine. He couldn't go home yet, not in his current mood. Besides, Sam was there and he couldn't face her right now. He needed time to think and come up with a plan, and there was no way he could do either with her in the house.

Out on deck, he buttoned his coat and turned up the collar to buffer the wind. Puget Sound was a calm, steely gray this morning, mirroring the sky, but there'd be a good breeze once the ship was under way. This was exactly what he needed to clear his head and think through the situation with Sam and his father.

James Harris had manipulated both of them and, as was so often the case, things had gone his way. AJ and Sam had stopped seeing each other, and neither had ever offered the other an explanation.

The horn sounded as the ferry eased out of the berth. He ignored the familiar announcements about safety and sifted through memories of what his life had been like before he'd "adopted" Will and severed ties with his family and the family business. He'd always been intimidated by his father, was sometimes downright fearful of him. They had never been a close family, but after his brother's death the rift between him and his parents widened considerably. His mother's drinking escalated. His father became even more controlling, expecting AJ to live up to the expectations he'd had for William. And AJ detached himself from his feelings because it was the only way to cope with the grief and the demands being made on him.

He leaned on the rail and watched the city's skyline pull away. Going along with his father had been a cop-out, he could see that now. He hadn't had to think for himself or make a decision—they were made for him. A college degree with a double major in business and journalism, followed by a high-ranking position at Harris Marketing and Communications, higher than any number of his father's longtime and dedicated employees, all of whom were infinitely more qualified for the job than he was.

And how he'd hated the business end of the job. All he'd wanted to do was write, but James Harris would have none of it. Someday his son would run the company from the corner office, not work in a cubicle with the nine-to-fivers.

A group of young people gathered nearby, and he found himself distracted by their laughter and easygoing banter.

Looking back, AJ could see he'd handled those expectations the way he managed everything else in his life. In spite of being angry and bitter, he quietly and unquestioningly went along with his father's demands and crammed a lid on his own dreams and desires.

And then along came Sam. In some ways she reminded him of himself, troubled and reserved. In others, she was a determined, take-charge woman who marched to the beat of her own drum. She was driving her destiny while AJ was adrift with his. Love at first sight sounded like such a cliché, but it's what had happened. He'd wanted to be with her, and he'd wanted to *be* her.

If he had told her he loved her, as he should have if he'd had any sense, she might not have believed what his father said to her. Instead, after she ended things with him, or at least refused to take his calls or have anything to do with him, he had shut down his feelings, the same coping mechanism he'd been using since his brother died. Then, when he discovered she was having his child, he'd done exactly what he hated about his father. He went behind her back to get what he wanted.

Last night with Sam had been a revelation. He hadn't fallen out of love with her when she left. He hadn't fallen out of love with her when he found out she was giving up her baby, his son. Angry with her, yes. Still in love with her, hell yes. That hadn't changed, at least not the being-in-love part, and the way she'd responded to his kiss last night strongly suggested the feeling was mutual. But with all the lies and deception, he'd dug himself a deep hole, and with every day he let the situation remain unresolved, the hole got deeper.

As the ferry cruised into Eagle Harbor and approached its berth at the Bainbridge Island terminal, he joined the other passengers making their way to the car deck. A few minutes later he was driving through town and then into the countryside. He'd always liked it here, had even considered moving here instead of to the cabin in the mountains, but at the time he thought it was too close to Seattle and the people he wanted to leave behind. That he'd come here to figure out a way to convince the most important person in his life to forgive him and let him back into her life, well, there was no mistaking the irony.

STRIPPING THE WALLPAPER in the living room turned out to be a much easier job than the foyer. "Lucky for me it's only one layer thick in here instead of three," she said to herself. "Here's hoping the same is true for the dining room."

She had filled several garbage bags with damp, tacky wallpaper and almost finished the second wall when William wandered in. "Hi, Will. Where's your nanny?"

He pointed to the dining room. "Working."

That's right. She was helping Kristi with the dusty clutter. "What are you doing?"

"Working."

Sam glanced over her shoulder and caught him crouching in front of her open toolbox. "Whoa, whoa, whoa. You can't play with those." She turned off the wallpaper steamer and set down the hose.

"I working."

"Are you a good worker?" she asked, holding his fingers out of the way and closing the lid.

He nodded so vigorously, his brown curls bounced.

He was so adorable, she wanted to hug him. "How would you like to be my helper?"

"I can help."

"Okay. See all this paper I'm taking off the walls?"

"Uh-huh."

"Well, all this paper has to get stuffed into bags, like this one. It's a pretty hard job, though. I'm not sure you're big enough to—"

"I'm big." He stood on his toes and held out his arms. "See?"

"Oh, my goodness, look at you. You're a very big

boy. I think you'll be perfect for this job." She lined a trash can with a fresh garbage bag. "Do you think you can pick up the paper when I take it off the wall and put it in here?"

"I show you." He scooped a piece of paper off the floor and put it in the bin, then peered over the edge, checking to see if it was in there. "See?"

"Very good, Will. You might be the best helper I've ever had." *And look at you, all motherly and everything.* Why had she doubted her ability to do this?

The little boy beamed up at her. "I a good helper."

She turned the steamer on and went back to work, keeping one eye on Will. For a little guy, he was single-mindedly intent on gathering up all the scraps of paper and putting them in the bag.

Several minutes later, Annie peeked into the living room, caught Sam's eye and gave her a thumbs-up. Will, focused on doing his "job," didn't even notice her, but Sam nodded back to let her know he was okay here and that Annie didn't need to worry about him.

She continued skimming the steamer nozzle over the wall, pausing every few minutes to tell Will what a great job he was doing, occasionally stopping to take her hammer out of her tool belt and pull out a nail she'd missed.

"I need tools," Will said.

"Do you? What kind of tools do you need?"

"A hammer, a saw an' a crew driver."

Sam smiled. "A 'crew' driver, huh? What would you build with your tools?"

"A house," he said without hesitation.

"You already have this house." Not for long, but she didn't know if he understood that.

"For Hawshey."

"Ah. It would be fun to build a doghouse." She could picture it at the back of the garden, a classic little dog-house with Hershey's name painted above the door. "What color would you paint it?"

Will scooped up an armload of wallpaper and seemed to give some thought to her question. "Brown," he said, dumping the paper in the bin. "Like Hawshey."

"Good idea. Maybe you and your father can build a house for him."

"Daddy hasn't gots tools."

This time Sam kept her smile to herself. She wasn't even sure why she'd said that since she couldn't imagine AJ building anything. He'd grown up in a family that didn't need to know how to build things or even do repairs. That's what hired help was for.

Sam was starting on the third wall when Annie reappeared. "It's lunchtime, and I'll bet the two of you have worked up an appetite."

"I helping Sam."

"I see that."

Sam turned off the steamer. "Even helpers have to take a break. Come on. Let's go wash our hands and see what's for lunch."

"Macaroni and cheese," Annie said. "Will's favorite. I just took it out of the oven."

He dropped his armload of paper on the floor and dashed out of the room.

Sam laughed. "Sounds delicious. I'll be right there after I finish cleaning up in here." If she didn't get the rest of the soggy paper off the floor, it would be dried up and stuck there when she came back after lunch.

In the kitchen, Kristi was packing the last of the now clean and dust-free plates from the dining room into a cardboard box. "Now I know why they call it a plate rail," she said with a grin. "There were forty-two of them."

"Wow. That's a lot of plates." And not one of them meant to be used for serving food. "Mmm. Lunch smells great."

"It does, and I wish I could stay but I just remembered I have to be at Jenna's school. I said I'd help with science fair setup." Kristi folded down the flaps of the box, sealed it with tape and labeled it with a black felt marker. "Ugh. Ten minutes ago," she said, glancing up at the clock. "Gotta run. I'll be back in about an hour and a half."

"No worries," Sam said. "We'll see you when we see you."

Sam washed her hands at the kitchen sink and dried them on a towel, and then she picked up Will and held him so he could wash his. "Scrub hard," she said. "You want to wash away all that wallpaper paste."

"What's paste?"

"It's the glue that sticks the paper to the wall."

"Glue is not for eating."

Sam laughed. That was a little nugget of wisdom to live by. "It sure isn't. That's why you want to make sure your hands are nice and clean for lunchtime."

He scrubbed hard, then she set him on the floor and handed the towel to him. "Do you need help with that?" she asked.

"I do it."

For a child who had a nanny and a stay-at-home dad to look after him, he was remarkably independent. He dried his hands as diligently as he'd washed them, and then she folded the towel and hung it up. She looked up and found Annie watching them.

"Here you go, young William. Your favorite, macaroni and cheese." She helped the little boy into his seat and waved Sam toward hers. "There's salad, too."

"Don't like salad," Will said.

Annie handed a little bowl of raw vegetables to him. "You, young William, get carrot and celery sticks."

"It's very generous of you to make lunch for me. When you said mac 'n' cheese, I was expecting the kind that comes in a box."

Annie tsked. "Homemade is always better. And it's no trouble, dear. I'm cooking anyway, so it doesn't matter if I'm feeding two or twenty."

Sam had never had to cook for more than two, so she wouldn't know. The top of Annie's casserole was crisp and golden, but the inside oozed with warm, melted cheese. Sam popped a forkful in her mouth and decided it was the closest thing to the perfect comfort food she'd ever tasted.

"I've noticed you always call him 'young William.' Is there an old William in the family?" She knew AJ was short for Andrew James, and that James was his father's name, but AJ had never mentioned anyone named William in the family.

"That's what Mrs. Harris always called him. He's named after Mr. Harris's older brother."

"Oh." AJ had an older brother? Sam searched her memory for any mention of him but came up blank. "I didn't know he had a brother."

"William died when he was a teenager. Tragic loss. Old Mrs. Harris liked to look at photographs of William and AJ, and she often talked about them. Those two boys were the apples of her eye, and she adored young William when he came along. Thought the sun pretty much rose and set on this little fellow, and used to say how much he looks like his uncle. Compared to the pictures I saw, I have to say she was right. All except for the eyes. Those aren't Harris eyes—he must get them from his mother."

More than once Sam had wanted to ask about her, and every time she'd talked herself out of it. What if she didn't like the answer? Still, if Annie knew something, Sam needed to know it, too. Feeling a bit like a paratrooper about to land in a minefield, she carefully chose her words and dove in.

"Does she come here often?"

"Never met her. If old Mrs. Harris knew her, she didn't ever let on, and Mr. Harris has never said a word about her." Annie poured some milk into Will's glass and slid the bowl of carrots and celery a little closer to his plate. "Eat your vegetables."

He nodded, his mouth too full of macaroni to speak, but he picked up a carrot stick in one hand, celery in the other, and waved them at each other like swords. No wonder his great-grandmother had doted on him, and that his father and his nanny still did. The eyes that weren't his father's sparkled with impish mischievousness. More than anything, Sam wanted them to be her father's eyes, her eyes.

"I've watched you with him this morning," Annie said. "You have a way with children."

"I do? Thank you." She took another mouthful of heaven and chewed.

Annie wiped a dribble of cheese off Will's chin. "You're a natural. You'll be a wonderful mother someday."

Somehow Sam managed to swallow the food in her mouth without choking. There was no way she could look Annie in the eye, so she stared at her plate instead. During the time she'd spent with Will that morning—

the walk to the park, keeping him occupied and entertained while she worked—she'd been totally in the moment. Now she was all but consumed by the regret for everything she'd lost.

"You're upset," Annie said. "What is it?"

Sam shook her head. "I'm sorry. It's just that…" She glanced at Will and quickly looked away. "It's nothing."

"I know nothing when I see it, and this isn't it. Has something I said upset you?"

"I *am* a mother. I mean, I had a baby but I gave him up for adoption."

In an instant Annie's hand was on hers, giving it a gentle squeeze.

What the hell are you thinking? Sam asked herself, immediately regretting her indiscretion. She had never told anyone about the baby. Not Kristi and Claire. She'd never even discussed it with her mother. Tildy had known about her pregnancy and the adoption—it would have been impossible to keep that from her—but she had never given the slightest inclination that she wanted to talk about it, and for that Sam had been grateful.

Why now? And why tell Annie, of all people?

Until now, no one had offered any comfort or support because she hadn't let them. Annie's hand was still on hers, and she liked it.

"I'm so sorry, dear." Annie's pale blue eyes were warm and reassuring. "That would have been a difficult decision for you to make, but when these things happen to teenagers, it's often the best one."

Sam stared at the remains of her lunch. "I wasn't a teenager," she confessed. "It was three years ago, but I was on my own and I already had my mother to look after and not much money and…well, getting pregnant was obviously a mistake. It was a mistake I had to live with, but it didn't seem right to make a baby pay for it, too."

Annie withdrew her hand.

Startled, Sam looked up and found the woman staring at her, hard. Her regret was immediate and profound. *Oh, no. What is she thinking? What was I thinking?*

But whatever Sam thought she saw in the woman's eyes, it was gone in a flash and once again she was the beneficiary of Annie's compassion. "Then your decision was an even harder one to make, but I can see you did it out of love. Love for your mother and your baby. No one can find fault in that, dear, and you shouldn't blame yourself, either."

Sam could hardly breathe. "Thank you," she said, the words barely audible even to her own ears. "That means a lot."

And then Annie's hand was back on hers. "Your baby boy is doing just fine. When I get a feeling about things like this, I'm always right."

Tildy was always getting a "feeling" about something and she was never right. Sam had learned to take them with a grain of salt, but Annie's "feeling"—she desperately needed to believe the woman was right.

"All done." Will's spoon clattered to the table and he squirmed to get out of his seat.

"You didn't finish your milk." Annie slid the glass toward him.

"Done," he said, shaking his head.

"All right." She helped him down from the table. "Let's put it in the fridge for your afternoon snack, then we'll wash your hands and face and have a story."

That, Sam knew, was the prelude to his afternoon nap. With Kristi gone, and Annie and the little boy upstairs, she could get back to work and some much-needed time to herself.

"Will you be okay?" Annie asked.

"I will." She had to be. She couldn't let the regret overwhelm her, she couldn't go back and change things, but if she was lucky enough to have a chance to make things right, she would grab it. She was disappointed that Annie didn't know who Will's mother was, but now she was more determined than ever to find out.

MOST PASSENGERS ON THE return trip from Bainbridge Island were taking advantage of the ferry's warm and comfortable lounges. AJ welcomed the solitude out on deck. It was already dark, except for a rim of purple in the western sky, and the city skyline sparkled against the blackness to the east.

He was ready to go home. After a day of soul-searching and considering all the consequences, he'd made a decision. He had to find a way to tell Sam that Will was her son. There was a chance she would never forgive him, might never speak to him again. Considering she barely spoke to him now and wasn't about to forgive him for things he *hadn't* done, that didn't feel like much of a risk.

She might try to get custody of Will. On the plus side, that would mean she wanted to be part of their son's life. The downside was that she might try to get sole custody, but he couldn't imagine a judge granting that. He was a good father and he could prove it; there was no way she could take his son away.

There was also a chance she *would* forgive him. Not right away, that would be too much to hope for, but in time she might. He hoped. If she did, they could work out some sort of arrangement, although if he had his way, they'd pick up where they left off in the foyer last night.

Slow down. He'd pretty much had things his way up to now, he reminded himself. He didn't get to decide what Sam's reaction would be, or how long it would take her to come around.

For now, Sam's reaction, whatever it might be, wasn't the most crucial thing. What was important was that he finally man up, stop acting like some pathetic carbon copy of his father and admit he'd made a mistake.

Sam had made mistakes, too. She had given up their child without even telling him the child existed, let alone that she didn't want it.

No, damn it. He wasn't going there. Especially not after finding out that James Harris had told Sam that AJ didn't want to have anything to do with her. Besides, he needed to focus on cleaning up the mess he'd made. Dwelling on other people's shortcomings was the kind of thing his father did. Only Sam could decide to make amends for the mistakes she'd made. He'd be plenty busy atoning for his own.

Reliving the feel of her in his arms last night had prevented sleep from coming. Tonight he hoped he would sleep. With a little luck he'd relive that kiss in his dreams, and it would be enough to keep him going until wishful thinking became reality.

Chapter Twelve

By the time Sam left for the day, AJ still wasn't home. Just as well. After her inadvertent lunchtime confession to Annie, her emotions were raw and she felt more fragile than the day she went home alone from the hospital. The nanny had steered clear of her all afternoon, and she'd made sure Will and the dog didn't interrupt her, either. Sam should have been grateful for that, but she had a hunch Annie was doing it because she felt sorry for her.

All afternoon she'd gone over their conversation and still had no idea why she'd blabbed the truth to a virtual stranger, especially one who worked for AJ.

What if Annie told him? Several times throughout the afternoon she had been tempted to track the woman down and ask her, beg her, *plead with her* not to tell him. Each time, she'd talked herself down, reminding herself that asking for Annie's discretion could just as easily have the opposite effect.

On her way home, she made a quick stop at the grocery store to pick up a few things for dinner and tomorrow's lunches, and while she was there she convinced the cashier to sell her a roll of quarters for the laundry. She was almost home when she remembered she had to swing by the building supply store to order new countertops for the kitchen and the bathroom vanities. She had taken the measurements that afternoon, and Kristi, who was starting to experiment with eco-friendly options, had chosen countertops made from recycled materials. Sam had a few reservations, but she'd learned to trust Kristi's instincts.

Inside, she made her way to the contractors' order desk. The clerk was leaning over the counter looking at a supply list, and she recognized the top of his balding head. "Hi, Bernie."

He straightened and looked at her over the top of his bifocals. "Well, if it isn't my favorite Ms. Fix-it. Haven't seen you in a while, Sam. What are you up to these days?"

"We're working on an old Queen Anne craftsman."

"Swanky neighborhood. What can I help you with this afternoon?"

"Countertops." She set her clipboard down and dug the sample out of her pocket. "Kitchen and bathrooms."

Bernie plucked a pencil from behind one ear. "I see you're going eco-friendly."

"Yeah, this was Kristi's idea."

"Good for her. We've been selling a lot of this product, especially for family homes. It's affordable, easy to work with, no toxic off-gassing. Made right here in the Pacific Northwest. Did you know that?"

She did not, but she was learning. She strove to do her best work, and now Kristi's top priority—turning a home into a safe, healthy and environmentally friendly place to raise a family—was starting to rub off on her. "You and Kristi should do a commercial," she teased, and handed the sheet of measurements to him.

Bernie laughed. "Listen, if you can get Kristi to agree to that, I'm in."

"I'll let her know. Any idea when these countertops will be ready?"

"Let's see." He poked a couple of keys on his computer keyboard and hitched his bifocals so he could read the monitor. "It's in stock at the warehouse. We can have it delivered on Monday."

"Perfect. The address is there on the sheet with the measurements, but the invoice goes to our office."

"Got it. Anything else today?"

"That's it for now. Thanks, Bernie."

On her way to the exit, a holiday display in the middle of the aisle caught her eye. Child-size open-topped toolboxes "for the budding builder on your Christmas list." Sam stopped to take a look. How cute were these? The box had a sturdy carrying handle and the wooden tools inside included a hammer, a saw with an exaggerated zigzag edge, pliers, a wrench and the requisite "crew" driver. The set seemed perfect for Will. The tools had smooth, rounded edges and were just the right size for a small child to play with.

She picked up one of the boxes and carried it to the checkout. How would AJ respond to her giving his son a gift? There was a chance that he wouldn't react favorably, but she didn't have to give it to Will now. She could wait until the work was finished and leave it with Annie to put under the tree.

Why are you doing this?

She just wanted to do something nice for him. She didn't need to have a reason. So she paid for the toy anyway and carried it out to her truck.

AJ RECEIVED AN ENTHUSIASTIC greeting from Hershey when he let himself in the back door. "Hey, fella. Sit." He held up his hand, palm out. "Hershey, sit."

Somewhat reluctantly, the dog lowered his haunches to the floor.

"Good dog." Training a dog required more patience than skill, it seemed, but they were getting there.

The kitchen was clean and quiet, indicating that Annie and Will had gone ahead with dinner instead of waiting for him. They'd be upstairs now, and the sound of running water suggested it was bath time. He opened the fridge and sure enough, Annie had filled a plate for him and covered it with plastic wrap. He was really going to miss this once he and Will were settled in the cabin, although after today the decision to sell this place and move to the mountains had less appeal than it had a month ago. A lot less.

He peeled the plastic off the plate and stuck his dinner in the microwave, then hung his jacket over the back of a kitchen chair. The room seemed a lot more spacious now that most of the clutter was gone. The curtains had been taken down, too. He remembered the Ready Set Sold women commenting on them the first day they were here. He couldn't remember what they'd said about them, probably because he hadn't cared then, and he cared even less now.

He was, however, curious to see what Sam had been working on today. Her truck was gone when he'd arrived, and that meant he could safely venture into the rest of the house without the risk of running into her.

The microwave dinged. He retrieved his plate and sat down at the table. Fried chicken with mashed potatoes and buttered peas, one of Will's favorite dinners. Both of them were going to miss this.

He'd spent most of the day driving around the island, had even skipped lunch, but he still didn't have much of an appetite. He ate it anyway—Annie would be offended if he didn't—and while he did, he sorted through his mail and glanced at the front page of today's paper. Nothing looked interesting enough to hold his attention. When he finished his meal, he put his plate in the dishwasher and went upstairs to say good-night to his son.

They were settled in the armchair in Annie's room with a storybook. Will, with his face framed by damp curls and cheeks still rosy from his bath, rested his head on her shoulder. He looked up with sleepy eyes and smiled.

"What are you reading?" AJ asked.

"Cars and trucks." He pointed to the page. "Fire truck."

Annie angled the book so he could see the cover. "It seems to be his current favorite."

"Sam gots a truck."

"She does. What did you do today?" he asked, looking to change the subject.

"I worked."

"Did you? What kind of work did you do?"

"I help Sam."

AJ noticed it was now just Sam and not Sam-I-am. And so much for changing the subject. He glanced at Annie, wondering if she would elaborate. She didn't. Instead she skewered him with her piercing blue gaze. He didn't know what that was about, but he had a hunch he'd find out as soon as Will was asleep.

"If you worked all day, that must be why you look so tired. Why don't you come with me and I'll tuck you into bed?"

Will yawned. "I take the book to bed."

AJ moved into the room and lifted his son out of the nanny's arms. "Say good-night to Annie."

"G'night." He yawned again. "Book, book, book…"

Annie closed the book and handed it to AJ.

"I've got it. Now let's get you under the covers."

"I'll go downstairs and make tea," Annie said. She didn't ask if he'd like some, and he knew better than to tell her he was in the mood for something stronger. That could wait until after she'd said whatever it was she was planning to say.

TILDY WAS SITTING AT THE kitchen table working on a jigsaw puzzle when Sam got home. She set the little toolbox on the kitchen counter and gave her mother a hug.

"What's that?" Tildy asked.

"What? This? Um, it's a toy tool set. A gift, for a… for a friend's little boy."

"You mean the baby you gave away?"

Sam staggered back and stared at her mother. Never, not once, had Tildy ever said a word about the baby. "No," she said, trying not to let her surprise come through in her voice. "Why would you even ask that?"

"It's the baby's birthday in a couple of weeks."

Her mother knew that? Sam couldn't remember the last time her mother had been lucid enough to carry on a conversation about something other than what was on television, what she was going to wear that day and which member of the royal family was coming for tea.

Did she dare hope the new medication was taking effect?

"You're right," Sam said. "I wasn't sure if you remembered."

Tildy looked up from the puzzle. Even she seemed a little surprised. "It just came to me now. Was it a boy or a girl?"

"A boy."

"Just as well, then. Boys can be a bother."

Sam couldn't have responded even if she knew how.

Her mother's interest was back on the puzzle anyway. "Did I tell you who came to tea this afternoon?"

"No. Who?"

"Elizabeth Taylor. Did you know that woman's getting married? Again?"

Sam didn't think her mother would want to hear that Elizabeth Taylor was dead. "I'm glad you had a nice time," she said instead. She didn't like to encourage her mother's delusions by acknowledging them, but she didn't feel guilty for doing it tonight. Sometimes it made life easier and besides, she already had enough on her conscience.

AJ SAT ON HIS SON'S BED AND waited until his eyes drifted shut before he turned out the lamp and reluctantly made his way down to the kitchen. He had a lot on his mind, but he'd better find out what Annie had on hers.

She was already seated at the table with the teapot beneath a patchwork cozy, a plate of shortbread, a cup and saucer for herself and a mug for him.

"I see you've been baking." He sat across the table from her and picked up a piece of shortbread. It was one of his favorites, and she knew it. Was she trying to soften him up for whatever she was about to say? He bit into the cookie and felt the sweet, buttery goodness melt on his tongue.

She filled the two cups with steaming tea. "I made these this afternoon while young William was napping. Did you have a good day?"

"It was...productive."

"Samantha took William and Hershey to the park this morning."

"Did she?" He hadn't expected her to start the conversation by mentioning Sam, and he'd be feeling more alarmed if not for her matter-of-factness.

"Then she kept young William busy for the rest of the morning, helping her clean up the wallpaper she was taking down."

Ah, that would be the "work" Will had talked about. AJ had assumed it was a fabrication, but apparently not.

"For a single woman without a family, she has a way with children, and I told her as much."

AJ adjusted his position in the chair and picked up his tea. It was still too hot to drink, so he set it down again. He'd wondered what she wanted to talk about, thought maybe she was going to give her notice because she'd found a new position. A conversation about Sam hadn't even crossed his radar.

Now she was waiting for his response and he decided that agreeing with her was the best strategy. "I've noticed."

"I thought you probably had. I invited them to have lunch with us again today. Kristi couldn't stay, but Sam did."

"Very thoughtful of you," he said, still watching what he said. It was an awkward conversation, and one he needed to navigate with caution.

"I enjoyed having the company and so did William. He's taken quite a shine to her."

AJ's uneasiness was quickly morphing into apprehension. Where was Annie going with this? "I've noticed that, too," he said.

"I'm curious. How long ago were the two of you... you and Samantha...an item?"

He considered telling her they never were, but she wouldn't believe him and might even consider it an insult. So he warmed his hands on his mug and met her gaze head-on.

"We ended things almost four years ago." Give or take. He still had no idea what the two of them had talked about over lunch, but the anxiety swelling in his gut suggested he was going to find out.

"I must have an honest face," she said. "People can't help confiding in me."

That comment made his skin go cold.

"Did you know that Samantha takes care of her mother? I gather the woman isn't well."

Okay, maybe he was wrong about where this conversation was going. And it was an odd coincidence that after the confrontation with his father that morning, the subject of Sam's mother's illness had come up again.

"Sam never said anything to me about her family but I thought that might be the case."

"Sam also told me she had a baby three years ago. Did you know about *that*?"

Wham. There it was, out of nowhere, his past catching up with him and hitting him upside the head like a two-by-four. He couldn't answer and didn't dare make eye contact, so he simply stared into his mug.

Annie calmly took several sips of her tea. "You probably want to tell me to mind my own business, but I think you should hear me out."

When he still didn't respond, she seemed to take that as a green light.

"Sam had a baby boy and gave him up. You have a little boy who doesn't have a mother."

"Do you think she knows?" He could scarcely believe this was happening. After an agonizing day of reflection and self-loathing, there was nothing he could do but wait for the other shoe to drop.

"I don't know. If she does, she didn't let on. If she doesn't, it won't be long before she figures it out. I'm telling you now because I love you and that little boy as if you were my own family."

She had figured out what he'd done, but she hadn't told Sam. A surge of relief took the edge off the fear and guilt that all but consumed him just a moment ago.

Annie calmly took another sip of her tea. "There's a natural connection between those two. I'm talking about the kind of tie that only exists between a mother and her child. Even though they don't know they're mother and son, the bond is still there, and it's powerful. If I wasn't seeing it with my very own eyes, I wouldn't have believed it possible."

He ran a hand through his hair. He had to be the one to tell her, and he would have to do it soon. "Please, Annie. Don't say anything to her. I will tell her, I was already planning to, but I need to do it my way, and when the time is right."

Her reluctance to go along with his request was obvious, and a little worrisome. "You know me," she said. "I'm no good about watching what I say, and I don't like walking on eggshells. I like having everything out in the open."

"I'll tell her. In fact, that's what I was doing today…"

"Deciding how you're going to break this to her?"

AJ drained his cup and pushed it away. "Yes, but I'm not quite there yet. I spoke to my father this morning and spent the rest of the day figuring out how to be less like him."

"What does your father have to do with this?"

"That's a long story."

Annie took the cozy off the teapot and refilled her cup. "I've got all evening."

AFTER SAM CLEARED UP THE dinner dishes and helped her mother settle in for the night, she hauled her laundry down to the basement. Luckily there was a free machine. She stuffed it with her dirty clothes, tossed in some soap and plugged the slots with quarters. Then she made her way to the storage room and opened the padlock on their storage locker. Last year she had stored some leftover Christmas wrapping paper and ribbon down here. Now she hoped the plastic bag she'd wrapped it in had prevented it from picking up the smell of damp must that pervaded the space.

Back in her apartment she opened the bag, relieved to find everything still in good condition. She chose a roll of paper decorated with cheery snowmen and cut a piece to fit the tool set she'd bought for Will. Where was the tape? She checked the odds-and-ends drawer in the kitchen. No luck. It wasn't in her room, either, which meant her mother must have it. She crept into the room, satisfied herself that the sound of her mother's shallow, regular breathing meant she was asleep and checked the top of the dresser. Sure enough, there it was. Tildy had used it to stick pictures cut from an old *People* magazine to her mirror.

Sam snuck back to the kitchen, wrapped the gift and tied the package with strands of red and green ribbon. In the bottom of the bag she found a gift tag with a snowman that matched the ones on the paper. For a long time, she sat with pen in hand, pondering what to write.

Finally she gave up on the sentimental drivel that kept coming to mind and wrote, "To Will. From Sam."

She still wasn't sure why she'd bought this for him, but she was sure he would love it, so she was glad she had. The question now was when to give it to him. The work on the house would be finished a couple of weeks before the holidays. Should she wait and deliver it at Christmastime? No. That would be too awkward. Better to take it on the last day of work, she decided. Kristi planned to put up a tree in the living room, so Sam could simply tuck the package underneath before she left. She had no idea how AJ would react. He might not even want Will to open it and if that was the case, she'd rather not know about it. And she had to avoid having to explain to AJ the reason for the gift, because she didn't have an explanation.

She put away the wrapping supplies and stowed the gift in her bedroom. The way AJ got under her skin and occupied her thoughts was dangerous on so many levels. She was in love with him and now she loved Will, too. The only thing she knew for sure was that there would be another broken heart, and it was part of a vicious cycle of her own making.

Chapter Thirteen

Sam arrived early for the weekly business meeting at the Ready Set Sold office, but Marlie was already at her desk and Claire was in her office. Both were on the phone. Sam took a chair, leaned back and closed her eyes. In spite of not sleeping well, she'd somehow made it through the past two weeks. All the work on the main floor was finished. There wasn't a scrap of wallpaper left, all the rooms dazzled with a fresh coat of paint, the kitchen's hideous linoleum had been replaced with a light neutral color and the new countertop was installed.

Kristi had decided to keep the pink-and-black color scheme in the second-floor bathroom. Much to Sam's relief. Tearing out and replacing all the ceramic tiles could easily have added another week to the job, and she was ready to put this behind her. Not that it made any difference, but she still kind of liked the bathroom the way it was. Instead, Kristi had stripped the room of crocheted ornaments, replaced the old vinyl shower curtain with a pretty white eyelet one, tossed the old towels and replaced them with fluffy white ones. Today Sam would swap out the drippy old faucet for a new modern one, and the room would be done.

After AJ's kiss she had recruited Kristi and Claire to

come to her rescue so she could avoid being alone with him. As it turned out, it hadn't really been necessary because it seemed that he was avoiding her, too. When he wasn't holed up working on his laptop, he was out of the house, usually with his son and the dog. Even Annie had been keeping to herself, although in all fairness, when she wasn't looking after Will, she was busy cooking, cleaning or filling the house with the scent of fresh baking.

"Good morning, angel. We're a bunch of early birds this morning." Marlie, just off the phone, already had her fingers tapping on her keyboard. Her color combination today was maroon and salmon pink. "Except Kristi. She called to say she's running five minutes late."

Or fifteen. Sam dropped an envelope with the week's receipts into the in-box on the corner of the office manager's desk. "Any messages for me?"

"No. Not even one from your mom."

At least not so far. "That's good. How're things going here?"

"Good. I'll just hit Send—" She rolled her chair back from her desk. "There. I'm all yours. Anything I can do for you?"

Sam rifled through the sheets on her clipboard until she found the one she was looking for, pulled it out and passed it to Marlie. "A couple of things, if you have time."

"For you, darlin', all the time in the world." She scanned the list. "Call the movers to reposition the furniture at the Harris home tomorrow. Put in a requisition to have the garbage bin hauled away sometime next week. Call the roofing company for an estimate on the Ferguson house. I haven't seen a contract for that one."

"They haven't signed one yet. The house is in pretty rough shape and they're still debating whether to fix it up or try to sell it as is. Claire thinks they'll have an easier time making that decision after she's shown them a couple of estimates for the major repairs."

"Makes sense. So this is it for you? Just these three things?"

"That's it."

Marlie added the list to a folder on her desk. "It's hard to believe someone who's so low maintenance is still single."

Sam laughed. "Who knew that was even possible? The low maintenance part, I mean." The being single part was a given. Besides, there was nothing wrong with being self-sufficient, especially since she'd never been able to depend on anyone else. "And it's not as though I'm the only single woman around here."

"Present company excluded." Marlie grinned and flashed her left hand.

"Holy moly. That's one very impressive girl's best friend."

"Thomas proposed on Saturday. We went out for dinner, and he had them put it in my tiramisu."

"How…romantic." To each her own.

Marlie giggled. "I almost ordered the crème brûlée. You should have seen the look on poor Thomas's face."

"I can imagine." She'd met Thomas only once. Her first impression was that he looked like a used-car salesman, and she'd been right. The ring-in-the-dessert move sounded right up his alley. What she couldn't imagine was pulling a diamond ring out of a dessert, dripping with marsala and marscarpone, and then… what? Licking it off and sticking it on her finger? Yuck.

"When I found it, he came around the table and got down on one knee, and popped the question. Then…"

Here it comes.

"…he licked the pudding off the diamond and slipped it on my finger."

Okay, this is way too much information. Especially since Marlie's version sounded even sleazier than the one she'd imagined. No wonder Sam's face was getting hot, and probably red, too.

"Everyone in the restaurant clapped, and the manager gave us complimentary glasses of champagne. It was so romantic."

"Nice. And I'm so happy for you," she added quickly. "Have you set a date?"

"Not yet, but what girl hasn't dreamed of a June wedding?"

And that would be me. She had never even imagined what a proposal might be like, although she now had a very good idea of what she didn't want to happen, never mind a wedding. Did that make her weird? Practical? More like resigned to the realities of life.

In lots of ways she was lucky. At least she hadn't married a deadbeat like Kristi's ex-husband. Or a cheating scumbag who left her for another woman, like Claire's ex. Or a man like her father, who simply got fed up and left. Ralph Elliott had signed on only for the "for better" and "in health" part of the package.

"Have to take this," Marlie said when the phone rang.

Claire was still talking and making notes, so Sam settled back into one of the two chairs in the corner of the reception office to wait for Kristi and watch Marlie admire her ring while she jotted notes on the pad in front of her.

Sam lowered her gaze to her own hands. Unadorned,

short nails, one of which was sporting a blood blister thanks to a misdirected hammer. They'd been polished only once. For Christmas, Kristi and Claire had given her a spa gift certificate for a manicure, and then nagged her until she finally made an appointment. The young aesthetician, horrified by the condition of her hands, had made it her mission to render the skin soft and the nails pretty. That had lasted until Sam's next workday. She turned her hands over and ran her left index finger over the calluses on her right palm. Not exactly the kind of hands that a man wanted to put a diamond ring on.

She glanced at Marlie, who was still on the phone and was now angling her hand this way and that so the ring caught the light from her desk lamp. Thomas, it seemed, had chosen well.

Kristi dashed into the office and deposited her bag on the corner of Marlie's desk. "Sorry to keep you waiting. Traffic's terrible this morning."

"No problem. Claire's still on the phone anyway."

"Not anymore," she said, popping out of her office. "And I won't make or take any more calls till after our meeting."

Kristi dropped a bulging envelope into Marlie's in-box.

Claire's eyebrows rose.

"Don't worry," Kristi said. "Those aren't all expense receipts. Most of it is inventory lists of all the items from the Harris house that I've taken to consignment stores."

"There was a lot of stuff in that place, but I dropped by the other day and I have to say, you've done an amazing job of clearing it out. Both of you have. I couldn't get over how airy and spacious the main floor feels now that the wallpaper's gone."

"Glad you think so," Sam said. "Just so you know, when we start the meeting I'm making a motion that we think twice before we take on another client with a wallpapered house. There were three layers in the dining room and each one was just as ugly as the one on top of it."

"Speaking of meetings, I'll grab my coat. I'm ready for coffee."

"And I'm starving," Kristi said. "No time for breakfast, but wait till you see the main-floor photos I took at AJ's place yesterday."

Claire pulled on her coat. "You were working on those this morning?"

"Late last night. I overslept this morning and that's why I didn't have breakfast."

"Then let's eat." Claire waved to Marlie. "I'll be back in an hour."

Sam followed her two friends out the door. Ten minutes later the three of them were settled at their usual table with their usual orders, Claire with her iPad, Kristi with her laptop and Sam with her clipboard and a pencil.

Claire sipped her mocha and set her cup back on its saucer. "First up is the Harris house." She gave Sam a hard look. "Everything going okay?"

"Everything's fine." At least everything with the house was fine, and that's what they were talking about. Once they moved past the business portion of the meeting, she had no doubt the less-than-okay stuff would be at the top of the agenda.

"Glad to hear it. Kristi, you said you already have photos. Let's have a look."

With the photos set to slide show, the three of them huddled over the laptop.

"The sunroom looks amazing."

"AJ uses it as an office, but I wanted to show how cozy it will be as a little getaway to relax with a book and glass of wine. So we scaled back on the desk and brought in these wicker armchairs."

Sam focused on the teddy bear, one of Will's, sitting on one of the chairs, and the photograph of the little boy displayed on AJ's desk. Kristi said they were nice touches in a family home. Sam thought so, too.

"The fireplace looks great, Sam. I know you weren't crazy about painting the brick, but the color Kristi chose is perfect."

"The proportions of the new mantel are perfect," Kristi said. "I can't wait to put out some of the Christmas decorations we found in the basement."

"You'll have to take more pictures when you do. I'll use some in the MLS listing."

Kristi clicked through the rest of the photographs and closed the program. "It's been a lot of work, but it's paying off big-time. This is shaping up to be our best project yet."

"Sam, anything to add?" Claire asked.

"It's going well. None of the unforeseen problems you'd expect to find in an older home." Way too many surprises with the home owner, but those were her problems.

She could tell Claire had questions about the home owner, but she'd also be the last one to break the "business before gossip" rule.

True to form, Claire glanced down at the list on her monitor. "Okay, next up. The Ferguson home. Where are we at with that?"

Relieved to change the subject, Sam dug out the notes she'd made during the quick inspection she and Kristi had done last week. "The roof is in terrible shape and there's already evidence of water damage to some of the ceilings."

Kristi brought up a new set of photographs on her laptop and turned it around to show Claire. "Sam's right. No amount of cosmetic work will cover this up."

"Marlie's going to call the roofing contractors this morning and have them give us an estimate. They're not that busy at this time of year, so we might even have that by tomorrow."

Claire was typing notes as they talked. "It's an estate sale, and to be honest I'm not sure how much the family's willing to invest in the place. If they decide against the new roof, what do you recommend?"

Sam shrugged and looked up from doodling on a blank sheet of paper. "They can price it accordingly and see if they can find a buyer, but I'm not willing to patch and paint the ceilings to try to cover up the damage."

"Absolutely not," Claire said, nodding in agreement.

"And honestly, it's not worth staging in its present condition, although I'll be happy to give the family a couple of pointers if they want to do the work themselves."

Claire stopped typing. "Okay. I'll ask Marlie to give me the estimate for the new roof and I'll show it to the Ferguson family when I meet with them later this week. I'll pass along your recommendations, too, and we'll leave it up to them."

Sam set down her pencil and picked up her cup. "Sounds like a plan." She swallowed some of the coffee. She hadn't been sleeping well, and the caffeine couldn't kick in soon enough.

Kristi nudged Sam with her elbow and grinned. "Anything else on today's agenda, or can we move on to the good stuff?"

Very funny. Serves you right for asking these two to cover your back.

"Just a couple of quick things," Claire said. "There's already been an offer on the Matheson place. The sale is pending the outcome of the inspection, but I don't expect they'll find any problems. And FYI, the agent who brought in the offer said the buyers *loved* the laundry room."

Kristi raised her hand and Sam gave her a high five.

Claire continued. "We got a call on Friday from a young couple who are expecting a baby in the spring and need more space. They want to sell their condo and buy something with more space."

"Condos don't usually need much in the way of repairs." Sam liked the sound of that, especially compared to the Ferguson place. She picked up her pencil and started drawing again. A small box with a triangle on top.

"That's right, but in this case I've already made one suggestion. I dropped by on Saturday to take a look at the place."

"You need to take a day off once in a while," Kristi said.

"It'd be nice if I had something to do besides work, but since I don't—" She polished off the last of her bagel. "About the condo. It has an open floor plan and lots of windows. Not a lot of square footage, but it has an amazing rooftop terrace. Wait till you see the views. Except for a couple of potted plants, the terrace is unused, so I suggested they add some custom-built furniture. It'll double the living space, and in the current market, especially for a winter listing, it'll really up the wow factor."

Kristi tapped the keys of her laptop. "How about

something like this? I came across these photos online last summer and bookmarked the site."

Sam examined the photos of an L-shaped cedar bench with a large square table. "Easy enough to build. Not sure about the cost, though. I'll have to see the place and take some measurements." She sketched some sides on the box she'd drawn, then added a door.

"I like it," Claire said. "All we need is something simple to give buyers an idea of how much potential there is out there."

"And you're sure they don't want to start till the new year?" Kristi asked.

"Positive. I've already told them we'll be closed for two weeks."

"Good," Kristi said. "Jenna was so excited when I told her I'd have the holidays off, I'd hate to disappoint her."

"What do you have planned?"

"We're going to Portland for a couple of days to visit my sister. Other than that, I plan to do lots of sleeping in. When I'm not supervising sleepovers and driving Jenna and her friends to the mall, that is."

"How about you, Sam?"

"Me? No plans. Spend some time with my mom, give Mrs. Stanton a break."

"What are you drawing?" Kristi had angled her head so she could see the page on Sam's clipboard.

Startled, she looked up, then back at her drawing.

Claire took a look, too. "Is that a doghouse?"

Apparently. She'd been listening to the discussion, though, and hadn't realized what she was doodling.

"Aw, it has Hershey's name over the door." Kristi gave her a playful jab in the shoulder. "Are you planning to build this for them?"

"No." Hell, no. "It's just a doodle."

The glances that passed between Kristi and Claire implied that they thought it was more than an absent-minded drawing.

"I'm *not* building a doghouse." She whipped the page from under the clip, folded it and stuffed it into the pocket of her jacket.

"How have things been going?" Claire asked. "Have you and AJ had any more close encounters?"

Kristi grinned. "Not with me playing chaperone."

"And not with me trying to avoid him."

"It hasn't really been necessary, though. He hasn't been around much. If I wasn't convinced that he still has a thing for Sam, I'd say he was trying to avoid her, too."

Really? Sam hadn't realized that. She stuck her pencil under the clip on her clipboard and closed the cover.

Claire put a hand on her arm. "Is that what you think?"

Sam shrugged. Why should it bother her if it was true? She had no idea, but it did. "As long as he stays out of my way, I really don't care how it happens."

"Pft. You do so," Kristi said. "I see you looking for him every time you walk into a room."

"Yeah. To make sure he isn't in it."

"Sweetie," Kristi said, "you might be fooling yourself, but you can't fool us. You've got it bad for this guy, and I see the way you are with his kid. He's got you wrapped around his little finger."

It was true, but not for the reason Kristi thought it was. She even had his Christmas gift stowed in her truck, ready to leave at the house on her last day of work. Worst of all, she still didn't know if he was her son, and she still hadn't confronted the lawyer. She wasn't sure what would be worse—finding out he was hers, or finding out he wasn't.

Oh, God. How had she let this happen?

"Is there really no chance the two of you could work things out?" Kristi asked.

"Not if they're avoiding each other." Claire's tone smacked of a conspiracy, setting off a red alert for Sam.

Kristi's eyes sparkled. "Now that we're finishing up the work on his house, they might want to replace business with a little pleasure—"

"No way, you two." She had been there, done that, and once was enough.

Another unspoken exchange passed between Kristi and Claire.

"I'm serious. Please don't go all matchmaker on me. There are things—" Things she couldn't tell them, not yet. Not even if it meant they would back off. She had already said too much to Annie. She'd made an appointment for the end of the week to see the lawyer who had handled the adoption. In her heart she already knew Will was her son, but before she confronted AJ, she needed proof. "Some things are best left in the past, and *this* is one of those things. Please, just let it go."

Kristi closed her laptop and gave her a hug. "You know we just want you to be happy."

"But we will let it go, won't we, Kristi?" Claire tucked her iPad into her bag and checked her phone. "Three messages. I'd better get back to the office."

Sam knew their hearts were in the right place, but she wasn't sure she completely trusted them to leave this alone, either.

Claire headed back to the office, and Sam walked

with Kristi to their parking spaces behind their office building.

"I'll see you at the house?" Sam asked.

"I just have to make one quick stop. I tracked down some drapes for a couple of the bedrooms, seriously on sale, and I need to pick them up. Do you think you'll have time to help me hang them this afternoon?"

"Of course." Were some of those drapes intended for AJ's bedroom? She hoped not. She had avoided going in there and she wanted to keep it that way.

THAT AFTERNOON SAM AND Kristi had the house all to themselves. After lunch Annie had taken Will to the library for holiday story time, and there'd been no sign of AJ all day. All the work on the main floor was finished, except the Christmas decorations that Kristi planned to put out, and the two of them had been working upstairs all afternoon.

"Have you got a few minutes to help me hang these drapes?" Kristi called from one of the bedrooms.

Sam set her wrench on the bathroom vanity. She had turned off the water to the sink so she could replace the leaky faucet with a new one, but since there was no one home needing to use it, it could wait.

"I'm on my way. I just need to go downstairs and wash my hands first."

Back upstairs, she found Kristi in the room that had been AJ's grandmother's, with several pairs of drapes spread on the bed and the rods spread out on the floor.

"There's new hardware?" Sam asked. "I thought we were just changing the curtains."

Kristi shook her head. "These old track-style rods are for pleated drapes, and new ones would have to be custom-made. Too expensive, so I went with these."

Damn. This was going to take a lot longer than expected, and she did not want to be up here when AJ came home. She buckled on her tool belt and hauled her stepladder into the grandmother's room. "I guess I'll start in here."

Kristi had set up an ironing board and was testing the iron to make sure it was the right temperature.

Sam had just climbed the ladder and was unscrewing the bracket when Kristi's phone rang. She didn't like the sound of her friend's side of the conversation.

"I'm so sorry," Kristi said after the call ended. "I have to go. That was the school. Jenna's sick—some kind of stomach flu thing—and they need me to pick her up right away."

"Will she be okay?"

"She'll be fine but I really need to get her home. Do you mind finishing these for me?"

"You want me to iron them, too?"

"Do you mind?"

She did, but she couldn't very well say that. "I'll finish the bathroom so I can turn the water back on, then I'll do these."

Kristi gave her a hug. "You're a lifesaver. There are just two pairs—one for this room and one for AJ's. We're keeping the ones in the nursery and the nanny's room."

Great. AJ's room was the one room in the house she did not want to set foot in. She'd do that one first, right after she finished with the bathroom sink, so she could be out of there before he got home.

The house was strangely quiet after Kristi left, so she turned on some music and plugged in her earphones to fill the silence.

She'd seen AJ's room that first day when they'd

toured the house, but she hadn't actually gone into it, and she'd been beyond relieved that Kristi said it was fine as is. Now she felt like a trespasser. The room was neat and the furniture was plain and solid, vintage if not antique. The nightstand held a lamp and a book, and she had to resist the urge to find out what he was reading.

On the desk in front of the window there was a wooden pencil holder, a neat stack of papers and a Ready Set Sold business card. The one with her name on it. The one she'd given him that first day? She wanted there to be some significance to its being there, and she didn't dare let herself speculate what it might be.

Get in and get out, she told herself.

She unfolded the ladder on one side of the desk, took down the faded old drapes—no wonder Kristi had decided to replace them—and dumped them in a pile on the floor. The old rod came down easily and she was relieved to find that the brackets for the new one covered the holes. She quickly threaded the new rod through the rings at the top of the new curtains, whipped it into place and stood back to take a look.

Much better. The beige linen looked fresh and made the room seem much brighter. She gathered up the old curtains. Kristi hadn't said what she planned to do with them, so Sam decided to take them into the grandmother's bedroom and leave them there with the ironing board.

She hustled out of AJ's bedroom with the armload of draperies, humming along to the music she was listening to, and ran head-on into AJ.

"Oh!" The fabric slithered out of her grasp as she put her hands up to steady herself. The warmth from his chest felt so good, like a crackling fire on a cold winter night.

He stared down at her, his hands gripping her arms, and all the emotions welling up inside of her were reflected in his eyes.

She tugged on a wire to remove one of her earphones. "You startled me. I didn't expect to see anyone...I mean...I didn't know you were here." She tried to back away but his grasp tightened, just a little, and his gaze intensified.

"AJ, I need to get back to work." She wished she meant it.

She expected him to say something, but he didn't. Instead his hands traveled up her arms and across her shoulders and then his thumbs caressed the sides of her neck, warming her skin and stroking her senses to life. Their gazes locked and he didn't have to speak because his eyes were telling her everything she needed to know.

He was going to kiss her, and she was going to let him. Too many things in the past had kept them apart, and once all those secrets were out in the open, they would prevent them from having a future together. Now, before everything *was* out in the open, she just needed to be with him.

His pupils dilated, turning his eyes a deep shade of cobalt, and he pulled her closer, letting her feel that he was fully aroused. His kiss was completely different from the last one, more urgent, with a raw edge. He kicked the pile of fabric out from between them and backed her against the wall. The world tilted, then rocked back into place. In the past their lovemaking had been passionate but always a little tentative, too, as though neither of them quite believed they deserved each other. This was a new AJ, more decisive, more determined, with a hint of ruthlessness that hadn't been there before. Bring it on. From the moment she'd walked in here a couple of weeks ago, she had craved his touch and ached for this connection.

The full-body contact, his hands on her body, the taste of him, fired an even deeper rush of awareness. For a split second she thought she shouldn't let this happen, should make him stop, but, oh, she needed this. Even more, she thrilled at the realization that he wanted her every bit as much.

Chapter Fourteen

After AJ kicked aside the pile of fabric—were those his curtains?—he briefly looked her up and down. Who knew a woman in a tool belt could be this sexy? He knew from experience where the buckle was and how to open it, and lowered it to the floor with a thud. Then, while her tongue eagerly responded to his, he pushed her shirt off her shoulders and tugged the bottom of her T-shirt up over her breasts, felt how the cool air raised goose bumps on her skin. Then, silencing the warning voice in the back of his mind, he backed her into his bedroom. She went willingly.

He had never been so turned on by a woman, not even her, and he couldn't get her clothes, or his, off fast enough. Even the work boots put up only a momentary roadblock, and then she fell onto the mattress with him and the bedsprings creaked. Good thing they were alone in the house because he intended to make those coils sing. Later, after they talked, if he was lucky enough to convince her to move in here with him and be part of this family, he was taking her shopping for a new bed.

Why was he thinking about lame-assed things like mattress shopping when Sam was under him and naked on this one? Her eyes, like deep, dark chocolate, stared up at him, telling him she was every bit as hungry for this as he was.

He rolled her onto her front, keeping one hand beneath her, pleasuring her, while he stroked one soft, succulent buttock. She squirmed and bucked, and the thought that she might be resisting this flitted through his mind, but her movements quickly settled into that timeless rhythm that took every man to the edge of self-control and left him teetering on the brink.

Her pace quickened and he matched it with his touch, loving that he could do this to her, have this effect on her, scarcely believing she would she let him. His blood thundered in his ears, leaving him mindless but with a heightened sense of awareness of every pulsating tremor that he teased from her. When her telltale pause indicated she was on the verge of an orgasm, he gently took her there. Her gasp and the guttural little groans played in his head like music, and for an instant he forgot his own need while he satisfied hers.

He rolled her back to face him, loving the way her eyes had softened. She was magnificent. He'd never get his fill of looking at her. Her breathing, still ragged, had her breasts taunting him. He massaged them lightly, sucked one stiff peak and then the other, but his control was waning fast. He kissed her again, thinking he couldn't get any more aroused, and she teased his tongue with hers, touching him lightly at first, then exploring deeply. He was done for.

He yanked open the drawer beside his bed, silently congratulating himself for stopping at the drugstore last week. In a flash the condom was in place, she had spread her legs to let him in, and he went. And came in a burst of glory, with her right there with him every step of the way.

There was a hint of a smile on her lips when he withdrew, and her eyes were closed. After a few seconds they fluttered open and focused on him. "You haven't said anything since I ran into you in the hallway."

He hadn't known what to say. *I love you?* There were other things he needed to say first. *I want to make love to you?* Too risky. She might have said no.

They lay together in an intimate tangle of arms and legs, damp and warm, and he still didn't know what to say, let alone what she needed to hear. "We've always been good together."

It wasn't what she wanted to hear. She sat up partway and he could tell she was looking for something to cover herself. She was looking for a way out, and he needed to find a way to keep her here. In a perfect world he would have told her everything she wanted to hear before making love to her. He was far from perfect, but he had to make this right.

"Sam, I'm sorry." He reached for her. "Don't go, please. We do need to talk…I want to talk…" He grappled for the words, not sure where to start, but knowing he needed her in his life, and so did their son.

The sound of footsteps on the main floor accompanied by voices—Annie and Will were home!—launched both of them out of the bed. He kicked his underwear under the bed and fumbled for his jeans while Sam scrambled to gather up her things. He managed to get his sweater back on, then reached for her.

"Take your time. I'll go downstairs and keep them distracted."

He pulled her into his arms, still naked except for

the panties, and kissed her. "This isn't over," he said. "We do have to talk."

He left her with that and went downstairs to sidetrack Annie and Will.

THE NEXT MORNING SAM CAME to work, not at all sure how she could face AJ after their clandestine encounter in his bed yesterday afternoon. AJ, true to form, wasn't there. Annie said he'd gone out and made some vague remark about having business to attend to.

Idiot. When are you going to learn that men like AJ use women like you for sex? All his talk about "needing to talk" was just that. Blah, blah, blah.

After lunch, though, Annie tracked her down. "Mr. Harris called. He said he hoped you'd still be here when he gets home."

"Kristi and I still have quite a bit to do, so I'm sure we will be."

"I think it's just you he wants to see."

Sam felt a flush on her cheeks.

"I'm guessing the feeling's mutual. I'll be taking young William out for the afternoon and that rambunctious dog is in the backyard, so the two of you will have the house to yourselves."

So, AJ did want to talk. Well, Sam didn't see the point.

She hauled her toolbox down the front stairs, set it by the front door and sprinted back up to get the rest of her things. In another hour, maybe less, she'd have everything loaded into her truck, and she would be out of here. Claire was coming over to help Kristi put up the Christmas decorations while Sam met the roofing contractors at the Ferguson house.

"Kristi, do you still need the stepladder up here or can I take it downstairs?"

"The ceiling fixture in the master bedroom still needs two lightbulbs." Kristi was in the bathroom, arranging apothecary jars filled with bath salts and cotton balls, and stacking coordinating towels on the open shelves Sam had installed the other day.

"I'll take care of that. Do you know where the bulbs are?"

"In the linen closet."

Sam grabbed a package from the closet and dragged the ladder into the master. She installed the bulbs and replaced the glass shades. A quick flick of the light switch to make sure they were working, which they were, and then she folded the ladder again and carried it back out into the hallway. She was halfway down the stairs, being careful not to scuff any of the fresh paint, when the doorbell rang.

Was Kristi expecting another delivery? Sam didn't think so, but she leaned the ladder against the wall and opened the door anyway, expecting to see a couple of delivery men with a last-minute addition to her partner's decorating scheme. Instead she was face-to-face with James Harris, AJ's father, the man who three years ago had threatened to ruin her life if she didn't stay away from his son. In the past three years, he'd aged at least six. His hair was grayer, the lines on either side of his mouth were deeper and his once prominent jawline was buried beneath a pair of jowls. Only the unruly eyebrows, now several shades darker than his hair, remained unchanged.

She started to back away, one hand gripping the door, ready to slam it shut on him.

"Wait," he said. "Please, Samantha, I was hoping to talk to you and my son."

Both of them? This made no sense. She knew AJ was on the outs with his father, and the man had long ago made it clear he had no use for her. So why was he here, and what was he up to?

"AJ isn't here, and I have nothing to say to you."

"Do you know when he'll be back?" he asked, ignoring the rest.

She shook her head and swung the door closed.

He blocked it with his foot.

She had a split-second debate with herself, whether or not to shout up to Kristi. She decided against it. The less she had to explain to her business partners, the better. Instead she lowered her free hand to the hammer in her tool belt.

His gaze followed the movement, and his eyes widened.

"I just want to talk." He held out a manila envelope as though it were a peace offering.

"I have nothing to say to you," she said, refusing to accept it, knowing better than to trust this man.

His Gucci-clad foot was still wedged against the door. "It's not what you think. It's a gift, a birthday gift for your son."

She would have been less stunned if he'd pulled a gun on her. He knew William was her son. William *was* her son!

He cleared his throat and continued. "After AJ came to see me last week, showed me the child's photograph...it forced me to do some soul-searching."

"Let me guess. You discovered you don't have one."

He looked away briefly, down at the envelope, and

then his gaze reconnected with hers and he held up the envelope a little higher, indicating she should take it.

No way.

"I deserved that," he said. "It must seem to you… and AJ…as if I don't care about my family, but I only ever wanted the best for them."

"And I'm not good enough, I get that." She pushed on the door, harder this time. "I'm not taking anything from you. You should come back when AJ's here." And I'm not.

"AJ doesn't want to see me, either. I suppose I can't blame him for that, but I want to leave this. It's not for you and my son, anyway. It's for William. For his birthday tomorrow."

She took the envelope because it was the only way she could think to make him leave. "I'll make sure AJ gets it." Then she shoved the door, hard, and this time he jerked his foot out of the way. The door banged shut and she flipped the dead bolt home, and then she sat on the stairs before her legs gave out on her.

She had no idea how long she sat there, or when the tears started, but she was still there and the crying was out of control when Kristi came down the stairs.

"Sam? Oh, my God! What's wrong?"

Kristi's voice and her footsteps on the stairs sounded far away, but then her friend was there beside her, and Sam was in her arms.

"What's wrong?" she asked again. "Is it your mom? Is she okay?"

Sam shook her head, then nodded.

"So she is, or she isn't?" Kristi asked, pressing tissues into her hand.

"She's…fine…" Sam said, releasing each word along with a sob.

"Then what is it? Sweetie, you're scaring me."

What was it? She was overflowing with three years' worth of grief and longing and love, and there was no way to make it stop.

"What's this?" Kristi held up the manila envelope.

Sam stared at it. "I don't know. AJ's father brought it for Will. It's his birthday tomorrow."

Kristi smiled at her. "I know. I saw the cake. What I don't understand is why that made you cry."

"James Harris."

"AJ's father? Is that who was at the door?"

Sam nodded. The tissue Kristi had given her was already soggy. "Got any more of these?"

"No, sorry."

"That's okay." She wiped her nose on her shirtsleeve.

"Okay, that's just plain gross. Let's go into the kitchen. I'll get you some more tissues and make some tea."

Sam was overcome by a fresh wave of panic. She had no idea when Annie and Will would be back, but AJ would be here soon. Right now she couldn't face any of them, especially not her son. Not until she got herself under control and figured out what to do. "No tea. I have to get out of here."

"Not so fast. You haven't told me what's got you so upset, and there's no way I'm letting you drive like this."

If Sam had an ounce of energy left, she would argue. Instead she let Kristi lead her into the kitchen.

"Sit." She disappeared into the powder room and reappeared a moment later with a box of tissue. After she plunked it on the table, she set the offensive envelope on the table next to it, then pulled out a chair and sat, knee to knee with Sam. "Spill. I'm not letting you leave till I've heard every last detail."

"No time." Sam plucked a fresh tissue from the box and blew her nose.

"Then how about starting with this?" Kristi held up the envelope. "What did AJ's father say about it?"

Sam grabbed another tissue and wiped her eyes. "He said…" She took a long, shaky breath and tried again. "He said that what's in the envelope is a birthday gift for my son."

"You have a son?"

The little energy Sam had left drained out of her. "It's a long story, Kristi. I can't talk about it now."

"Is it AJ's baby? It's not…oh, my God. Is it William?"

Sam could only nod.

Kristi squeezed her hands. "So all this time you've been working here…why didn't you tell us?"

"I didn't know. At least not at first. Then I suspected…" She dried her eyes and spilled out the details of James Harris's threat and realizing she was pregnant. "It was so hard, giving him up after he was born, when all I wanted to do was hold him—"

"So AJ found out you were pregnant and…wow. Sweetie, you have to talk to him."

The thought of talking to him now set off a fresh new wave of panic. She jumped up, spilling crumpled tissues from her lap onto the floor. "Not while I'm like this. I have to go home."

"Okay, okay. Would you like me to drive you?"

"I'm fine."

Kristi put her arm around her shoulders and walked with her to the front door. "I think you're forgetting something."

"What?"

"Sam." Kristi's voice was barely audible. "There's a certain little boy here who's already crazy about you."

William. He really was her son. She had anticipated this moment for weeks, yet was totally unprepared for it. She had expected to be wildly happy, but instead the future felt less certain than ever. The worst part was not knowing how AJ would react when he discovered that his secret had been revealed. She had to pull herself together before she saw him because now that her son was back in her life, she wasn't letting him go.

Chapter Fifteen

Sam stumbled into the apartment, greeted by the blaring television. Her mother was ensconced on the sofa, remote in hand, the remnants of her lunch still on the TV tray next to her.

"Hi, Mom. I'm home a little early."

Tildy didn't look away from the screen, and Sam was grateful for that. Saved her the trouble of fabricating an explanation for her puffy, red-rimmed eyes. Her mother was wearing one of her favorite dresses, a brown-and-purple paisley sheath with a draped collar that had been in her closet since before Sam was born. It was one of the dresses that often accompanied a delusion, and if there was one thing that could take an already crappy day right down the sewer, that would be finding out the new meds weren't working.

Slow down, she warned herself. *Maybe it's not as bad as it looks.* "How was your day?" she asked. "Did you have any visitors?"

"No. I just felt like dressing up," Tildy said. "You are early. You usually don't get here till after *Jeopardy* comes on. And why are you galumphing around in those boots?"

She'd hung up her jacket but forgotten to take off

her boots, and of course her mother would notice, even though she never "galumphed." Not wanting to alter their routine any more than necessary, Sam sat next to her and gave her a hug. "We finished ahead of schedule so I came home early. I'm going to get changed and go out for a run. Is there anything you need before I leave?"

"No. Mrs. Stanton brought lunch. Oh, look. I like this commercial."

The conversation came to a stop while a department-store commercial played across the screen, promising viewers a sleigh-load of savings.

"While you're out you should pick up some milk," Tildy said after the ad ended. "We're out again."

Sam very much doubted that. "Sure thing, Mom. I'll make dinner when I get back."

"What are we having?"

Sam stood up and heaved a sigh. Her heart was pounding, her head was throbbing and she could barely string together a coherent thought, let alone come up with a plan for dinner. "I'm not sure. Let's talk about it when I get back."

On the way to her room, she stopped by the bathroom for a couple of aspirin. Not that they would remedy this kind of killer headache, but they couldn't hurt. She washed them down with a mouthful of water straight from the tap, grabbed a box of tissues off the back of the toilet and took those with her.

In her room, she closed the door, pulled the curtains and sat on the bed to take off her boots. For a few seconds she was tempted to crawl under the covers, work clothes and all, and stay there. Giving in to her feelings meant rethinking and reliving everything that had happened in the past few weeks—having AJ back in her life, finding out that Will really and truly was her

son—her son!—and now having to accept that she'd
been deceived by her lawyer and by the man she loved.

Thinking about it hurt too much, and the only way
she knew to make it go away was to hit the streets and
run until she was numb with exhaustion. Before she left
the building, she would stop across the hall and prevail
upon Mrs. Stanton to fix her mother's dinner because
she didn't know how long this was going to take.

AJ STOOD IN THE FRESHLY refurbished sunroom that
now—to use Kristi's words—did double duty as a place
to work and to relax. Right now he wasn't doing either.
He'd spent the better part of the day quietly making ar-
rangements for Will's birthday tomorrow. He'd decided
tonight would be the night he'd talk to Sam, tell her the
truth and hope that she would still be here tomorrow to
celebrate their son's birthday.

All day he'd rehearsed what he would say, but by
midafternoon when he got home, Sam's truck was gone.
After days of working well into the evening, there was
no sign of her—no toolbox, no tarps and paint cans,
nothing. Now Annie and Will were home from their
shopping expedition and had gone upstairs to wrap gifts
to go under the tree, and Sam's two business partners
were putting the finishing touches on the house. The
banister in the foyer was festooned with holiday gar-
lands and big red velvet bows, and the two women were
now decorating the tree in the living room. Today was
supposed to be their last day of work, tomorrow the
for-sale sign would go up, and Claire would hold the
first open house the day after that.

He'd asked Annie to have Sam wait for him. Sam
had obviously ignored that request. Now there'd be no
reason for her to come back, and he couldn't believe he

had missed her. He needed to move on to Plan B, and he would, if he had one.

To add to the puzzle, he encountered two unexpected items here in his office. A gift-wrapped Christmas present and a large manila envelope, both for his son. The tag on the gift indicated it was from Sam. He didn't feel right about opening it, so he set it aside. If his plan played out as intended, Sam would give it to him.

The envelope was another matter. It had a business-like weightiness to it, and it must have been hand delivered because it hadn't come by mail and there was nothing to indicate a courier. Since when did three-year-old boys receive what appeared to be a package of legal documents? Since Will couldn't read, and since AJ's curiosity was getting the better of him, he grabbed the letter opener off his desk and slit the flap.

He read the covering letter twice before it sunk in. The papers were from his father's lawyer, outlining a trust fund set up in Will's name, a gift for his third birthday. Enough to cover four years of college tuition and expenses. The summary sentence suggested the gift was given with no strings attached.

Bullshit. Everything from his father came with strings attached, usually in the form of dire threats or unrealistic expectations. He also had an uneasy feeling that Sam's disappearance might be directly connected to the appearance of a hand-delivered package from his father.

Should he go up and ask Annie if she knew what had happened? No. He couldn't have that conversation in front of his son.

Call Sam and see if she would talk to him? Definitely not a conversation he wanted to have over the phone.

It would be too easy for her to hang up on him, if she bothered to answer.

He could call his father, except that was a conversation he didn't want to have at all.

That left the two women in his living room. From what he'd seen, Sam, Kristi and Claire were more than business colleagues. They were close friends, and most likely confided in one another. Would they answer questions about Sam? He had no idea, but it was worth a shot. Hell, at this point it was his only shot.

The Christmas decorations flowed seamlessly from the foyer to the living room. The tree was ablaze, the mantel had been decorated with greenery and more lights and there was a log ready to be lit in the fireplace. Through the French doors, he could see Kristi and Claire in the dining room, spreading a tablecloth on his grandmother's antique oak table. He opened the doors and went through.

They both gave him a wary look when he walked into the room, a dead giveaway that something had happened, they both knew what it was and he probably wasn't going to like it.

"The house looks great," he said.

Kristi smoothed a wrinkle in the tablecloth. "Thanks."

"Thank you," Claire said, her voice crisp and overly professional.

"No, thank *you*." And he meant it. He'd had his doubts, but even a man who didn't like to worry about appearances could see that the house would now have much more appeal to buyers. Just when he was having serious second thoughts about selling it.

"Well, you're welcome," Claire said, sounding a little abrasive. "Kristi and Sam have done an amazing job, like they always do."

With those pleasantries out of the way, he carefully chose his next words.

"I'd like to thank Sam in person. Do you know when she'll be back?"

The two exchanged a quick glance.

Kristi shook her head.

Claire shrugged. "She won't be. Something came up and she had to leave early."

"I see."

"Would you like us to pass along a message?" Claire really was all business now.

"I'd rather speak to her in person. She left a Christmas gift for my son. I'd like to thank her for that, too."

If either woman was surprised to hear about the gift, they didn't let on.

"I was also wondering if one of you was here when a package arrived this afternoon—an envelope, actually, addressed to my son. I need to know who delivered it."

The pair exchanged another look.

Claire lifted his grandmother's holiday centerpiece out of its box and set it in the middle of the table. "Sorry," she said. "I don't know anything about it."

Kristi stopped fussing with a pile of napkins. "I think we should tell him." In spite of a warning glare from her colleague, she met AJ's gaze head-on. "I didn't see the man who delivered the envelope, but Sam said it was your father. He said something to upset her, and she went home. That's all I can say, though. If you want to know anything else, you'll have to talk to Sam."

She went back to folding napkins and all of Claire's attention was focused on the centerpiece. There was no question they both knew more than they let on, a lot more, and nothing he could say or do would drag it out of them.

"Thanks," he said before leaving the room. "I appreciate your honesty."

There were still more gaps than facts, but he now knew enough to guess what his father had done. AJ had been worried that Annie might inadvertently say something about Will before he delivered his confession to Sam, but it hadn't occurred to him that his father would show up here and ruin his life, again.

He took the stairs two at a time, and found Annie and his son in her room amidst a mass of wrapping paper and ribbon.

"You're back," Annie said, deftly tying a bow from a length of ribbon. "I'll be starting dinner soon."

"Daddy, I see Santa today!" Will came flying at him from across the room.

AJ reached down in time to catch him, swinging him up and into his arms. "Are you sure it was Santa? He's not supposed to come till Christmas Eve."

Will giggled. "It was him. He has a beard."

"I hope you don't mind," Annie said. "We were at the mall and there he was. Will wanted to line up with the other children waiting to see him."

"Don't mind at all. I'm glad you took him." With everything he'd had on his mind lately, it never would have occurred to him. "What did Santa ask you?" he asked, running a hand over his son's unruly curls.

"What I want for Christmas."

"And? What did you tell him?"

"A house for Hawshey an' a toolbox…like Sam."

Like Sam. AJ's chest went tight. After yesterday he'd been thinking—no, wishing and hoping were closer to the truth—that he and Will might get Sam, tools and all, for Christmas. Today he wasn't so sure.

Annie smiled up at them. "Santa told him to be a good boy and he'd see what he could do."

"I *am* good, an' now I helping." Will held up both hands to show strips of tape stuck to each finger.

"Helping with the tape, I see." AJ put him down and watched him rejoin Annie.

"He's a very good tape dispenser," she said, smiling at Will's eagerness. Her smile faded when she looked back at AJ. "Is everything all right?"

"Something's come up," he said. "I have to go out again and I hate to ask, but would you give Will his dinner and put him to bed for me? I don't know how long this will take."

"Of course I don't mind." She plucked a piece of tape from Will's hand and used it to attach the bow to the gift she was wrapping. "I put a couple of things in your office. Sam left a package, and there was an envelope that came while I was out."

"Saw them, thanks." He shoved his hands into his pockets, debated whether or not to ask, then decided he had nothing to lose. "Did you happen to see Sam before she left?"

Annie looked up again and drilled him with her gaze. "No. She was already gone when we got home. Did you speak to her?" Her question was layered with double meaning.

"Not yet."

"Off you go, then. And good luck. We'll see you when you get home." She peeled two more strips of tape off Will's fingers. "You'd better say good-night to your father."

"Good. Night." Will flapped his fingers and tape at him, mercifully oblivious to everything that was at stake.

"See you in the morning, son. Thanks again," he said to Annie, and took the front stairs back down to the foyer. He pulled on his overcoat, and before he left he went back into his office and brought his old briefcase out of its retirement in the bottom drawer. The envelope from his father went inside, then he retrieved a small packet of photographs from the top drawer. That, he hoped, would be his trump card. He tucked it into an inside pocket, grabbed his keys and left the house, as ready as he would ever be to face his future.

Chapter Sixteen

Sam trudged up the two flights of stairs to her apartment, shaking raindrops off her windbreaker as she went. The long, hard run had cleared her head, and she had reached a decision. Tomorrow she would talk to a lawyer. Tonight she was emotionally and, after running for hours, physically drained. All she wanted was sleep. With any luck, it would come the instant her head touched the pillow.

She pushed through the door to the third-floor hallway. Mr. Kirkpatrick's cigar smoke mingled with Mrs. Babiak's cabbage and the disgusting combination rushed through her heightened senses and filled her freshly inflated lungs, almost making her gag. She tugged the lanyard with her apartment keys over her head and quickly stuck the key in the lock.

With the door not yet closed behind her, she heard voices, and they weren't TV voices. She stopped and listened. Her mother. Mrs. Stanton? Why was she still here? Sam tossed her key onto the table. "Mom? I'm back. Is everything—?"

She rounded the corner to the kitchen and… What the hell?

Tildy sat at the kitchen table, radiant in red lipstick

and even more rouge than she'd had on earlier, presiding over the teapot, and her guests. Two very *real* guests, sat across from her—Mrs. Stanton and AJ Harris.

"There you are," her mother said. "I told everyone you'd come home sooner or later. You remember my friend, Elizabeth Stanton, and this…" Tildy gave them all one of her rare smiles. "This is Prince Andrew. He's come for tea."

AJ was watching her, and if her mother's nonsensical introduction even registered with him, he didn't let on.

Sam opened her mouth to say something, and closed it again when nothing came out. *Prince Andrew?* What the…? Of all the royals Tildy had been known to entertain, she'd only once before mentioned Prince Andrew. Had he been here before? Is that how he knew about the baby?

Sam whirled around and reached for the doorknob. She was soaked with rain and perspiration, weak with hunger and exhausted beyond belief. No way could she deal with this tonight.

AJ caught her before she made it to the hallway. "Sam, we need to talk."

"Not now, AJ. Go away and leave me alone."

"I talked to my father. I know what happened this afternoon."

"Do you? Well, I wish *I* was talking to your father right now because that's how much I *don't* want to talk to you."

He led her into the hallway and closed the door. "Then I'll do the talking. All you have to do is listen."

She lowered her voice. "In the hallway? While all my neighbors have their ears to the doors?"

She tried to go back inside, but he stopped her.

"You'd rather do this in front of your mother and her friend?"

"I'm not doing this tonight. I can't."

"I'm not leaving until you've heard what I have to say. Damn it, Sam. Do you think this is any easier for me?"

That's the best he could come up with? "You think I give a rat's ass about how difficult your life is?"

He ignored that and took her arm, his grip a little gentler this time. "If you don't want to talk here, we'll go someplace else."

"Outside. On the sidewalk. That's as far as I'll go." She jerked her arm out of his grasp and started for the stairway. "And you'd better make it fast."

At least he had the good sense to keep his mouth shut while he followed her down the stairs and outside.

She stopped in the circle of light beneath the street-lamp. The rain had picked up, so she pulled up the hood of her windbreaker. It wasn't completely waterproof, but she'd be drier than he would be. She faced him, keeping her distance and avoiding eye contact.

"Sam, I know you must hate me right now, and how can I blame you? But I was going to tell you about Will. I never expected you to find out like this. You have to believe that."

"I don't *have* to do anything. And when were you going to tell me? After you moved to Idaho and took him away from me again? When he was ready to graduate high school? College? You can think again because I'm meeting with my lawyer tomorrow."

She looked him square in the eye to see how he'd react to that, and was satisfied to see it had hit the mark.

"We're not going to Idaho."

That stopped her for a moment. "Then where? Some-place even farther away?"

"We're staying in Seattle."

"Oh."

"I want you to be part of his life. Our lives. It was never my intention to 'take him away' from you. I thought you didn't want him, but I did."

Sam looked down at her feet, not wanting him to see the tears filling her eyes. "I wanted him more than I've ever wanted anything, but I was on my own, I didn't have a lot of money and what I did have was spent on looking after my mother. After he was born I almost changed my mind." She looked up then and waved a hand at the windows of her third-floor apartment. "But I couldn't raise a child here, like this. It wasn't fair to him."

"Why didn't you tell me you were pregnant?"

"You didn't want me, so why would you want my baby?"

"Our baby. And I never told you I didn't want you. You're the one who ended our relationship."

"Your father threatened me, said you didn't want to have anything to do with me."

"I didn't know he'd done that until a couple of weeks ago, that night in the foyer, when you fell off the ladder."

The night he'd kissed her, and she'd discovered she was still in love with him.

"My father lied to you."

"So if you really didn't want to end things, why didn't you ever try to contact me?"

"Because he lied to me, too." AJ ran a hand over his damp hair. "Can we go inside? Or at least sit in my car?"

Right now the thought of being trapped in an enclosed space with him brought on a rush of panic. "No. If you still have things to say, then you can say them here. Or you can leave."

"Fine. Fine, we'll talk here. There are things you don't know about my father. Mostly that he's never been a very nice person."

"Oh, I think I figured that out."

AJ was shaking his head. "My older brother committed suicide when he was sixteen. I'm the one who found him."

Annie had told her about the brother who died, but she had not said anything about suicide. Hearing it now, knowing that AJ had been the one to find his dead brother's body, took the edge off her anger. "I'm sorry. His name was William, too."

"How did you know that?"

"Annie told me. I assumed it was an accident."

He shook his head. "It was no accident. My father did his best to make it seem like one, though. We...my mother and I...were never allowed to talk about it. Like that was going to change what had happened." From the bitterness in AJ's voice, his brother's death might have taken place yesterday. "So I started to cut off connections to family and friends, and my mother made new ones. Pills and booze."

She didn't know what to say, but that seemed okay because he wasn't finished talking.

"My grandmother was the only person who ever let me talk about what happened. I still let my father run the show, though. He told me what to study at college, and I did. He wanted me to join the family business, so I did. He wanted me to marry the right woman."

This was a side of AJ she'd never seen. He was a man of few words. Hell, she couldn't ever remember them having a conversation that lasted this long, and he'd never come close to letting on what he was feeling. "I envied what you had with your family," she said.

"The Harrises are nothing if not masters at keeping up appearances. But I envied you because you were doing what you loved, and you were so good at it."

She wasn't ready to reach out to him, but she wanted him to know how sorry she was. "I wish you had told me about your brother. I've had a little experience with people who suffer from mental illness."

"You never told me about your mother, either."

He was right. They'd both kept their share of secrets. "I've been protecting her and covering up for her since I was a kid." That's something else she was really good at.

"My father found out about her."

"I know. He told me she belonged in an institution."

He shook his head. "He never told me about her. I didn't know until I came to see you, after I found you were having my baby. You weren't here, but I talked to her and she told me you were giving the baby away because you didn't want it."

"She told me about that visit, but she said you were Prince Andrew, so I didn't think it was real. My mother is…" She still hated saying it. "Sometimes her reality isn't the same as everyone else's."

"I know, but that's okay." For the first time, he smiled. "I kind of like being called a prince."

That made Sam smile, too. "How did you find out I was pregnant?"

"I saw you leaving the lawyer's office. Melanie Morrow works for the firm that handles my father's company business."

"How did you know the baby was yours?"

"Because of the timing. For the baby not to be mine, you would've had to be sleeping with someone else while we were together. I knew you well enough to know that wasn't possible. And…" He looked down at the sidewalk as though he didn't want her to see what he was feeling. When he looked up again, his composure was back. "And because Melanie asked you to have a blood test."

She remembered that. The *adoptive family* had wanted to be sure she and the baby were healthy. "So she knew it was your baby?" God, did she even want to know how he got the lawyer to go along with him? She was sure of one thing. Money would have changed hands.

"I've done things I'm not proud of, but I won't apologize for them. Will is my son. *Our* son. If I hadn't done what I did, neither of us would have him now." AJ paused and brushed the rain off his hair. "That's not a reality I like to consider."

Images of Will examining her tools, helping her pick up scraps of wallpaper, playing in the yard with his puppy, tumbled through her mind. "He looks like you, but he has my father's eyes."

AJ nodded. "Your eyes. It's one of the things I love most about him."

She wasn't ready to hear him say things like that. Not yet. "From that first day, I felt connected to him, and it was weird because I've never spent any time around small children. I thought it might be because—" There were things she wasn't ready to say, either.

"Because…?"

She would have to say them sooner or later, though. Maybe this was a good time to get it over with. "Because he was yours. Because I've always regretted my decision. Because if you and I…if we reconnected, there was still a chance we could be a family. At first, though, I thought you would never forgive me if I told you what I'd done. But then Annie mentioned Will's birthday and it seemed like too much of a coincidence to really be one."

He tugged her hands out of her pockets and held them. "And I've spent the past few weeks trying to figure out how to tell you that he's your son, too."

"Why did you wait so long?"

"Because I thought you'd never forgive me. But then yesterday, you let me make love to you and I figured I had a shot. So I spent today meeting with the lawyer and arranging to sell the place in Idaho."

"So you really plan to stay in Seattle?" She had to ask, although she knew he meant what he said.

"We're not going anywhere." Again he brushed the rain off his hair. "You left a gift for Will. What is it?"

"A set of tools."

He laughed.

"I didn't mean for it to be funny."

"It's the opposite, actually. I think it's…serendipitous. That's what he told Santa he wants for Christmas. 'Tools, just like Sam's.'"

"Really?"

"He's crazy about you. In fact, I'm pretty sure he'll be the happiest little boy in the world when we tell him you're his mom."

"You're going to tell him?"

"I hoped we could tell him together."

Sam's heart opened up then, and the love that poured out of it overwhelmed her. No matter what happened between the two of them, she had found her son and AJ was letting her into his life. With her eyes brimful of tears, happy ones for a change, she looked up at him. "I couldn't ask for a better Christmas present."

He pulled out the envelope he'd tucked into his pocket. "This is for you. Another early Christmas present. Don't open it out here, though. They're photographs. You won't want them to get wet."

She knew without asking they were photographs of Will. She quickly tucked them into her pocket for later.

AJ put his hands on her shoulders. "Speaking of presents, Will asked for one more thing."

"What?"

"A doghouse for Hershey."

Sam brushed away more tears. After the business meeting that morning, she had stuffed her drawing of a doghouse into her pocket. She dug it out and unfolded it, angling the page so it caught the light from the streetlamp, not caring that it was instantly dappled with raindrops. "What do you think?"

"I think it's perfect, I think you are going to be an amazing mother and I don't think I've ever loved you as much as I do right now."

"You love me?"

"I love you. I've always loved you."

She thought having her son for the holidays was the sweetest gift possible. She was wrong. Those three words, spoken out loud by the only man she'd ever loved, were the icing on the cake. The frosting on the gingerbread house. Her smile turned into a giggle, and she flung herself into his arms. "I love you, too."

"And that's making you laugh?"

"No, it's making me happy." She'd tell him about the gingerbread some other time. Right now she was all talked out. Besides, there were other things she'd rather be doing. Like kissing the father of her child. And kiss him she did.

Epilogue

Sam stood in the kitchen, gazing through the doors that led to the deck and the backyard. *Her* backyard, she reminded herself. This would take some getting used to. AJ came into the room and stood behind her. She leaned back against his chest, secure in the circle of his arms, more sheltered than she had ever felt in her life.

"What do you think?" she asked.

"He's going to love it."

She tipped her head to the side so she could look up at him. "I think he will, too."

"I'm sure Hershey will, too, once he gets used to it."

"It's too big to bring inside, and there's no way it'll fit under the tree anyway."

AJ crossed his arms over hers. "The doghouse looks great out here. You're amazing, you know that? It looks *exactly* like the sketch you drew, and I can't believe it only took you a day to build it."

"The lights were a nice touch." Those had been AJ's idea, and Sam thought they were the perfect finishing touch to the house she'd built for Will's dog. "So he'll open the gifts under the tree first, then we'll bring him outside and surprise him?"

"Sounds like a plan."

"Where is everyone?" she asked. After dinner they'd made a big production of putting out milk and cookies— gingerbread men—for Santa. Then while she'd been outside stringing the lights on the eaves of the doghouse and installing Hershey's new bed inside, AJ had taken their son upstairs to read him a bedtime story.

"Will's out like a light. I thought he might be too excited to sleep, but he could hardly keep his eyes open."

"And Annie and my mom?"

"Upstairs in your mom's room, having tea."

A lump rose up in Sam's throat. After years of sheltering her mother, worrying about upsetting her routine, the move had scarcely had an effect on her, except in a positive way.

"My father called to wish us a merry Christmas. He wondered if it would be okay if he and my mother dropped by tomorrow."

"What did you tell him?"

"That I needed to talk to you first."

"They're your family, AJ. Of course they should be here. And we still haven't thanked them for Will's birthday gift."

"It's that easy for you to forgive him?"

"I've spent a lot of years blaming other people for the way my life turned out. I don't want to waste any more time doing that. I don't want there to be any more regrets and I really don't want there to be any more secrets."

"No more secrets." AJ put his arms around her and kissed her, and Sam forgot about everything except how wonderful it felt to love, and be loved.

* * * * *

HEART & HOME

Heartwarming romances where love can
happen right when you least expect it.

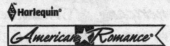

COMING NEXT MONTH
AVAILABLE DECEMBER 6, 2011

#1381 BIG CITY COWBOY
American Romance's Men of the West
Julie Benson

#1382 A RODEO MAN'S PROMISE
Rodeo Rebels
Marin Thomas

#1383 A BABY IN HIS STOCKING
The Buckhorn Ranch
Laura Marie Altom

#1384 HER COWBOY'S CHRISTMAS WISH
Mustang Valley
Cathy McDavid

REQUEST YOUR FREE BOOKS!
2 FREE NOVELS PLUS 2 FREE GIFTS!

Harlequin®

American ★ Romance®

LOVE, HOME & HAPPINESS

YES! Please send me 2 FREE Harlequin® American Romance® novels and my 2 FREE gifts (gifts are worth about $10). After receiving them, if I don't wish to receive any more books, I can return the shipping statement marked "cancel." If I don't cancel, I will receive 4 brand-new novels every month and be billed just $4.49 per book in the U.S. or $5.24 per book in Canada. That's a saving of at least 14% off the cover price! It's quite a bargain! Shipping and handling is just 50¢ per book in the U.S. and 75¢ per book in Canada.* I understand that accepting the 2 free books and gifts places me under no obligation to buy anything. I can always return a shipment and cancel at any time. Even if I never buy another book, the two free books and gifts are mine to keep forever.

154/354 HDN FEP2

Name _____ (PLEASE PRINT) _____

Address _____ Apt. # _____

City _____ State/Prov. _____ Zip/Postal Code _____

Signature (if under 18, a parent or guardian must sign) _____

Mail to the **Reader Service:**
IN U.S.A.: P.O. Box 1867, Buffalo, NY 14240-1867
IN CANADA: P.O. Box 609, Fort Erie, Ontario L2A 5X3

Not valid for current subscribers to Harlequin American Romance books.

Want to try two free books from another line?
Call 1-800-873-8635 or visit www.ReaderService.com.

* Terms and prices subject to change without notice. Prices do not include applicable taxes. Sales tax applicable in N.Y. Canadian residents will be charged applicable taxes. Offer not valid in Quebec. This offer is limited to one order per household. All orders subject to credit approval. Credit or debit balances in a customer's account(s) may be offset by any other outstanding balance owed by or to the customer. Please allow 4 to 6 weeks for delivery. Offer available while quantities last.

Your Privacy—The Reader Service is committed to protecting your privacy. Our Privacy Policy is available online at www.ReaderService.com or upon request from the Reader Service.

We make a portion of our mailing list available to reputable third parties that offer products we believe may interest you. If you prefer that we not exchange your name with third parties, or if you wish to clarify or modify your communication preferences, please visit us at www.ReaderService.com/consumerschoice or write to us at Reader Service Preference Service, P.O. Box 9062, Buffalo, NY 14269. Include your complete name and address.

HARIIB

Lucy Flemming and Ross Mitchell shared a magical,
sexy Christmas weekend together six years ago.
This Christmas, history may repeat itself when they find
themselves stranded in a major snowstorm...
and alone at last.

Read on for a sneak peek from
IT HAPPENED ONE CHRISTMAS
by Leslie Kelly.

Available December 2011, only from Harlequin® Blaze™.

EYEING THE GRAY, THICK SKY through the expansive wall of windows, Lucy began to pack up her photography gear. The Christmas party was winding down, only a dozen or so people remaining on this floor, which had been transformed from cubicles and meeting rooms to a holiday funland. She smiled at those nearest to her, then, seeing the glances at her silly elf hat, she reached up to tug it off her head.

Before she could do it, however, she heard a voice. A deep, male voice—smooth and sexy, and so not Santa's.

"I appreciate you filling in on such short notice. I've heard you do a terrific job."

Lucy didn't turn around, letting her brain process what she was hearing. Her whole body had stiffened, the hairs on the back of her neck standing up, her skin tightening into tiny goose bumps. Because that voice sounded so familiar. *Impossibly* familiar.

It can't be.

"It sounds like the kids had a great time."

Unable to stop herself, Lucy began to turn around, wondering if her ears—and all her other senses—were deceiving her. After all, six years was a long time, the mind could play tricks. What were the odds that she'd bump into *him,* here? And today of all days. December 23.

Six years exactly. Was that really possible?

One look—and the accompanying frantic thudding of her heart—and she knew her ears and brain were working just fine. Because it was *him.*

"Oh, my God," he whispered, shocked, frozen, staring as thoroughly as she was. "Lucy?"

She nodded slowly, not taking her eyes off him, wondering why the years had made him even more attractive than ever. It didn't seem fair. Not when she'd spent the past six years thinking he must have started losing that thick, golden-brown hair, or added a spare tire to that trim, muscular form.

No.

The man was gorgeous. Truly, without-a-doubt, mouthwateringly handsome, every bit as hot as he'd been the first time she'd laid eyes on him. She'd been twenty-two, he one year older.

They'd shared an amazing holiday season.

And had never seen one another again.

Until now.

Find out what happens in
IT HAPPENED ONE CHRISTMAS
by Leslie Kelly.
Available December 2011, only from Harlequin® Blaze™

LAURA MARIE ALTOM
brings you
another touching tale from

When family tragedy forces Wyatt Buckhorn to pair up
with his longtime secret crush, Natalie Poole, and care
for the Buckhorn clan's seven children, Wyatt worries
he's in over his head. Fearing his shameful secret will
be exposed, Wyatt tries to fight his growing attraction
to Natalie. As Natalie begins to open up to Wyatt,
he starts yearning for a family of his own—a family
with Natalie. But can Wyatt trust his heart enough
to reveal his secret?

A Baby in His Stocking

Available December
wherever books are sold!

SUSAN MEIER

Experience the thrill of falling in love
this holiday season with

Kisses on Her Christmas List

When Shannon Raleigh saw Rory Wallace staring at her
across her family's department store, she knew he would
be trouble...for her heart. Guarded, but unable to fight
her attraction, Shannon is drawn to Rory and his inquisitive
daughter. Now with only seven days to convince this
straitlaced businessman that what they feel for each other
is real, Shannon hopes for a Christmas miracle.

Will the magic of Christmas be enough
to melt his heart?

Available December 6, 2011.

www.Harlequin.com

HRI7769

ROMANTIC
SUSPENSE

USA TODAY BESTSELLING AUTHOR

MARIE FERRARELLA

Brings you another exciting installment from

CAVANAUGH
JUSTICE

A Cavanaugh Christmas

When Detective Kaitlyn Two Feathers follows a kidnapping case outside her jurisdiction, she enlists the aid of Detective Thomas Cavelli. Still reeling from the discovery that his father was a Cavanaugh, Thomas takes the case, thinking it will be a nice distraction…until Kaitlyn becomes his ultimate distraction. As the case heats up and time is running out, Thomas must prove to Kaitlyn that he is trustworthy and risk it all for the one thing they both never thought they'd find—love.

Available November 22 wherever books are sold!

www.Harlequin.com

HRS27753